After the Stranger Came

Frederic Lindsay

After the
Stranger Came

ANDRE DEUTSCH

For Alison

First published in 1992 by
André Deutsch Limited
105–106 Great Russell Street
London WC1B 3LJ

Copyright © 1992 by Frederic Lindsay
The author has asserted his moral rights

CIP data available from the British Library

ISBN 0 233 98779 7

Printed in Great Britain by
Billings Book Plan Limited, Worcester

It was the back end of the year when the stranger met me on the hill called Scad Law, thanked me for putting him on the path and went down to the village. Though I didn't spare him a glance as he went, a man like any other, our great-grandfathers would have found a name for him. Not that I believe in the Devil any more than you do; that thought came to me only because of what happened later. All any of us can say for certain is that everything was all right before.

There was no trouble until after the stranger came.

Gibson's *Twentieth Century Folklore*

Minding

'Why are you doing this? I won't listen to this.'

'Well, you watch then,' he said, and took the nipple of the girl's left breast between his finger and thumb. As he twisted and wrenched it, an expression of disturbance rather than pain altered her features.

'You're all right,' he told her, and at once the look passed from her face.

'I've seen that before,' one of the other men said. 'It's his parlour bleeding trick.'

There were two of them. As far as he allowed himself the idea of friendship, the Garage Owner was a friend, the closest one he had. The Minder though was a stranger, brought along without a by your leave, which showed the limitations and dangers of friendship. Not much more than twenty, uninvited, he had stepped in with a shrug of the shoulders as if conferring a favour. In his own eyes, it seemed, he had East End prestige – his connections being good to the families that mattered; he hinted at a death presently rumoured to his account. Watching the girl naked from the waist up, however, sweat gleamed now on his forehead and marked the line of the scar that ran from his upper lip.

Sweat, you cocky young bastard!

'Have you seen this before?' he asked the Garage Owner. 'Seeing as you know all my tricks.' He spoke to the girl firmly, but not loudly, in the tone of ordinary conversation. 'Open your eyes, Sleeping Beauty. Have a look at your tit – the other one, stupid!' Obediently, her gaze shifted to the one he held by the tip. As he worked on it, she watched without any sign of response.

'Jesus Christ!' the Minder said. 'It's not natural. She must be fucking mental.'

'Not her,' he said, sly, triumphant, almost offended. 'You'd rate her, meet her in her gear out on the street. Smart girl, got class. She wouldn't give you the time of day.'

But he had gone too far. His stomach tightened with apprehension as the Minder touched the scar's disfigurement, scowling with a dark immediate anger. He hurried on. 'What I'm saying, all I'm saying is, she's not stupid. But she believes what I tell her.' What I'm saying, all I'm saying is, you bastard, I've got power. 'That's all there is to it. I mean there's no magic to it.' But could not resist adding, 'If you know how.'

'Could you show me?' the young man asked. The scar on his cheek shone white against the flush of his skin. 'How to – how to put somebody under like that?'

Instead of answering, he said to the girl, 'Let's play dogs. Down you go.' With eyes still open but unfocused, she went down on hands and knees. 'Wag your tail.'

The Garage Owner burst into laughter. With some difficulty because of his bulk, he bent over her and curved his fingers into her buttocks. At the touch, she winced forward until the only voice she could hear ordered, 'Stay! The nice man wants to pat you. Good dog.' At that she was still, supporting herself on hands and spread knees,

2

her head hanging down as if in shame as the fat man pumped his hand against her. Only since he was the one who decided, how could she feel shame? A puppet having its strings pulled. He had some funny ideas come into his head. In the stillness, the fat man's hand made faint rasping noises against the material of her jeans.

The Minder dropped to his knees beside the fat man. On his feet looking down on the two of them crowded against her, as much as her they appeared to him as animals.

His expression altered as the young man looked up. 'Can I touch her?' he asked. 'She isn't going to come round?' At his shake of the head, the young man put out his hand and tentatively took a grip on the breast that hung nearer him. He took it gently, cupping its softness in his hand.

Without taking his eyes from what he held, he said, 'She's a slag, knows what she's doing, must do. You're not making her, not really.'

Cocky young bastard! what was he talking about? he knew nothing of the power.

'You're a lucky bitch,' the voice told her. 'You're at the dog show, yes you are. The judges are going over your points. They're really going over them. Find out what kind of bitch you are. It wouldn't surprise me if you were in line for the first prize. Wag your tail, go on, give us a bark.' As she moved against him, the Garage Owner groaned with pleasure; but at the double note of the broken cry she gave the young man snatched his hand away in guilty fright.

'First prize!' the Garage Owner wheezed, wriggling his bulk against her. 'I've got it here, I'm going to give it to her.'

'I think you might get a prize from all the judges,' he said, looking down on them. 'Tell you what – you need a pee first – lift your leg and do it like the dogs.'

As the fat man cursed and bumped back, the girl cocked up a leg. Urine's sharp stench twitched their nostrils and a stain spread on the crotch of her jeans and darkened along the thigh.

'That's a bloody liberty, that is,' the Garage Owner complained. 'You're an unhygienic bastard.'

'Don't worry,' he said. 'They're due off about now. And when we've finished with her, she'll clean up the mess.'

'She can clean up the crap with a toothbrush. That's a trick I could learn her,' the Minder said, laughing. The girl's indignity had released him from his inhibitions.

'Finished with her?' the Garage Owner cried in his high fat man's falsetto. 'Who's talking about being finished with her? We haven't bleeding started on her. It'll be a long time before we're finished with her. A long time before I'm finished with her.'

'With anybody?' he repeated and struggled between vanity and caution. 'I can put other people under. Course I can. But – I'm not denying she's a bit special.' They stared at her where she crouched on the floor wiping with a piece of rag at the stains on the carpet. About all of them there was an air of satiety like men who had eaten too well. 'She was my bit of luck. I'd gone to this office—'

'This knocking shop, he means,' the Minder said.

'She was only sixteen. My mouth watered when I saw her. I got her talking. She was having a bad day, and me – I was travelling in drugs then—'

'Ladies' underwear, you mean,' the Minder said. 'You was travelling in ladies' underwear.' The Garage Owner wheezed a chuckle, indulging him.

'I was practically a doctor.' He winked. 'She trusts me – that's the secret. I send her a letter and she meets me. I don't just bring her here, you know. We've eaten up West and one time I had her for the weekend at Brighton. But I put the blocks in, don't I? She don't remember anything I don't want her to.'

'She won't remember any of this?' the Minder's friend asked. 'Not what we've done?'

'Put it this way, she hasn't so far – and I've used her regular these last three years. Got a fair bit of cash out of her as well. For medical treatment. Her folks give it her. One time they got a bit stroppy about the cost and I told her she'd a paralysed hand. She couldn't straighten it out. Not until they gave her something to get it treated. Now she's on a better earner she pays her own way. Well, it's worth it, isn't it – to keep healthy?' With only a touch of parody, he shifted to the accent of a different class. 'There's no waiting list, of course, not like the bloody National Health – she's a private patient.'

'What about those? What happens if somebody sees those? Her mother or somebody?'

'She's not usually marked,' he said drily. The Minder frowned and glanced away. 'I'll tell her to be careful nobody sees them. Not even the boy friend.'

'Boy friend?'

'Course she has. Pretty kid like that. She's due to get married.'

'That'll spoil your game.'

'Why would that be? I don't know anything about him, but if he's flush I just might carry on with the treatment. Put the price up, shouldn't be surprised. Love's young dream, he wouldn't grudge it.'

'Dodgy.'

'Don't see why.'

'Dangerous for you I mean.'

'She does whatever I tell her. Maybe he's the one would have to be careful.'

'It would depend who he is,' the Minder said. 'You wouldn't want to pick on the wrong guy.'

Such vileness! It has nothing to do with us. You have no right.

*

5

At the noise he seized up as if paralysed and then when he relaxed the sickness came up sour into the back of his mouth. He dropped the shirt into the case. On top he threw shoes and the electric razor in its box. Stranded helpless then, he tried to think. Time was running out for him.

At first he had paid no attention to the man sliding on to the vacant stool beside him at the bar. More than a month had gone by since the night with the girl, but more than the time that had passed, it was the state of the Minder that prevented recognition until he spoke. His face had been carved and beaten out of shape.

'I met her again,' he said. 'That little girl of yours. Funny thing is — I knew the bloke she was with. And, don't laugh, I told him. I'd been feeling bad about it, you see. And there was a time when him and me were by way of being mates. You're going to think I'm a real cunt — I wanted to make it right. I told them I'd pay you a visit myself, but they didn't want that. Him and her brothers took their time explaining that to me. And here you are still alive.'

'I've been out of town,' he said stupidly.

'I reckon they're going to fucking kill you the slowest way. And I'll come to the funeral. I wouldn't miss seeing you going into the ground.' He stood up and moved the ruins of his face in what might have been rage or grief. 'You should have found out who her boy friend was, you stupid bastard.'

He stared into the case, not able to think what else he should take. Somebody had been in the flat. Though they had been careful, he had seen the signs. Once they heard he was back — He had to get away. But where?

'All the faces looking for you,' the ruined man sneered. 'You can't hide.'

BOOK ONE

The Good Wife

1

It was the act of a good wife. If she did not go, it was true, he would still catch a connection within the hour; and even so early, probably he would be able to get something to eat while he waited. All the same, anticipating the pleasure of his surprise, she rose early with a good conscience, taking credit from the warmth of the bed she was abandoning of her own free will and finding the crisp clear air of a fine morning almost a disappointment.

Fields and hills unwrapped themselves from the darkness as she drove, and coming into Edinburgh it was light. In Princes Street, she ducked her head to catch a glimpse of the old castle on its plug of rock, memento of a spent volcano. Flushed clouds in red and orange framed it: dramatic, obvious, a bit of a cheat . . . All of that, but still she could for once, alone in the car at dawn on a November morning, enjoy it without bothering too much about its past or present. She enjoyed it for what it seemed to be. It rose in the cold air as a piece of theatre. People forgot that here you were north of distant Moscow. Or was it if you were in Aberdeen? Not that it mattered. Someone had told her that. She smiled and in her imagination the castle tipped, a giant absurd samovar, pouring tea over the ranked chimneys of the New Town and its Sunday sleepers.

She had this ridiculous sense of making a beginning. She laid claim to the cold bright morning by right of virtue and early rising. The gaudy clouds flew a banner over the castle for her by way of promise.

Yet she was only going to meet Maitland – whom she loved, of course, no doubt of that – but whom after all she had met in the mornings and evenings of so many days; a lifetime ago jumping off a bus at the stop near her parents' home; striding through the gate from an international flight (giving her his private signal of relief, Maitland hated flying); very often like today off a train, returning from a meeting, from a conference. It was a tribute to Maitland that she should still be capable of feeling this lift of excitement; surely it was a tribute to their relationship; anyway, it said something about her, about the youthfulness of her heart.

It was annoying that the train should be late.

'I had no chance to check,' she explained. 'I left home so early.'

The girl in the brown coat, who had given her the bad news, nodded. 'I was even worse – I was so afraid of being late I was too early even if it had been on time. I hardly slept.'

'Poor you,' she said seriously.

They walked together past the newspaper kiosk where they were laying out the first bundles of early editions and turned along by the side of the booking hall. The girl pointed to a sign which read STATIONMASTER. 'We can ask there for when it's due,' she said. 'The porter told me to ask there.'

'Who are you meeting? Your boy friend?'

The girl laughed self-consciously. 'No one exciting. Only my brother. He's coming up from Bristol.'

'I'm meeting my husband – Professor Ure.' She looked at the girl, for a moment expecting her to respond, then laughed and explained, 'My husband isn't on the faculty at Edinburgh. There's no reason why you should know him. It's just that at home all the students do, you see. And for some reason, I assumed you were a student.'

She paused and glanced at her companion for confirmation, but the girl said nothing. 'I suppose it's because at

10

home almost all the young people I come into contact with are students.'

'I hope someone is here,' the girl said, and they turned into the Stationmaster's office.

A counter separated them from the dingy interior. A young man in his early twenties leaned on a table and muttered into the phone. Diligently he ignored them. She disapproved of him – of his shirt-sleeves, of the ear-ring, even of the rims of red flesh from which his eyes peered; he would revenge himself on them by means of an ingenious ignorance. When he finished, however, he was pleasant and even, within limits, helpful. It struck her that the girl was pretty. Very pretty.

In fact – not a student, only a stranger after all – admit it, the girl was almost beautiful.

'Not too long,' the girl said. 'Not as bad as the porter made out.'

'They like a bit of bad news to pass on.'

'Do you think so?' The girl shook back her hair, a movement which would have been natural if it had been worn long, but with a crop cut short seemed affected. Perhaps it was a style she had taken to only recently. 'I thought he was all right.'

'Once he detached himself from the phone.'

'From the phone? No, the porter – I meant the porter.'

And neither of them smiled at the confusion. Normally, she would have, she was sure of that. The difference she felt came from the girl. The girl seemed to her with that habitual gesture, as if shaking back long blonde hair, and those moments when her pretty features went quite blank with self-absorption, someone whom it would be easy to dislike.

At once, she reproached herself with being unfair.

'I must get some Sunday papers,' she said. 'After travelling, my husband will be looking forward to a quiet afternoon.'

In the kiosk, she gathered up *Scotland on Sunday*, the *Observer*, the *Times*, and went back with them to the car.

Piling the fat wads of sections like bricks into the boot, she saw how the newsprint had streaked her hands with dirt. For a vague staring moment, she wondered how many trees had been pulped to make this bundle laid neatly to one side to leave room for Maitland's luggage. Leaves bunched and rising towards the light ... living things needing to survive at any cost ...

As she crossed the concourse, people began to stream around the corner of the booking hall towards her. Leaning against the weight of cases, they had the crumpled appearance of overnight travellers. That fool of a man's got the time wrong, she thought. I'll miss Maitland; he'll be into a taxi and gone before I find him. She was swept by a flush of anger and then by a panic so excessive it made her afraid. If she missed him, it wouldn't be the end of the world. When she got back, they would laugh about it. It would become one of Maitland's stories, and then but more richly she would be a sharer in the event. As for blaming any of it on the girl, what could be more unreasonable? Yet if she had been alone, she would not have chosen that moment to go for the papers. It did seem, after all, as if it was the girl who had spoiled mysteriously all the morning's bright anticipations.

She saw Maitland first and then with an unpleasant little shock the girl and that he was talking to her. The third figure in the group registered only vaguely; a man, and one smaller in stature than either of his companions.

Seeing her, Maitland smiled and waved. 'Always faithful,' he said. 'My wife Lucy,' he said to the girl; and then to her, 'Miss Lindgren tells me you've already met.'

'Miss Lindgren? But how – Didn't you say—'

'Oh, yes.' The girl smiling covered her mouth with her hand for a moment. 'You guessed right when you thought I might be a student. Actually in one of the Professor's classes. I've always been lucky.'

'But your brother?' The last stragglers were lingering up from the platform. In a moment, their little group would be left behind alone. 'Oh, of course,' and she smiled at the man full of the warmth of relief, 'how obtuse of me. This gentleman must be—'

All three of them joined in the laugh against her: the man, the girl Miss Lindgren, even Maitland.

'Nobody's brother,' the man said. 'Sorry.'

At that she saw him properly for the first time; thick dark hair and ugly-attractive face, rather dark complexion; and it seemed for a moment that he might have been introduced as a brother not of the girl but of Maitland. The resemblance was there, and then it blurred, for the stranger at best was too ordinary – merely a life-size version of Maitland, she thought, and smiled. Yet his voice caught her attention; a very deep voice, carefully resonant, and with the faintest shading on the vowels that seemed to echo back to a childhood somewhere in the English countryside. Devon came into her mind, a place with which she was unfamiliar.

'This is Michael Norman. We became acquainted last night, neither of us feeling like sleeping.' Maitland swept out his arm as if embracing the stranger. 'We've half decided I'm going to alter his life.'

'Monty,' the stranger said. 'My friends call me Monty.'

He struck her then as being common. It was like Maitland to gather up some stranger out of a humdrum journey on a train. I'd have snoozed all night – or pretended. I would have hated sharing with someone I'd never met before.

Instead she had slept in her own bed, dozing and starting awake in case she overslept. Now suddenly, looking at them smiling, she was the one who was tired as if at the end of a journey.

'Your brother,' she said to the girl, 'wasn't he on the train? Did he miss his connection? From Bristol, was it you said?'

Infuriatingly, the girl shook back her hair, went again through the same pantomime. 'Oh, not on this train,' she said. 'Not on this one.' And she smiled brilliantly. 'Not coming from Bristol.'

13

Miss Lindgren seemed to be one of those girls who suffer a personality change in the presence of men. She longed to tell her, They won't think any more of you for simpering like an idiot. Nor much less of her, she added honestly – not when you're as pretty as this one is.

'We can't offer you a lift then,' Maitland was saying to the girl, so firmly that it seemed he too had had enough of her, 'not if you're waiting for your brother.' That settled, he turned to the man – what had he called him? Norman. Michael Norman. Monty – 'to his friends'.

'But you'll come with us?'

'I could walk – The station here's right in the centre of the city, isn't it? Maybe you could recommend a place?'

'Not to an hotel,' Maitland said impatiently. 'Come back and have breakfast with us. We've plenty to talk about still.'

Glancing back on some impulse, she saw Miss Lindgren as left behind and disconsolate. The impression was so clearly a trick of the imagination that she dismissed it at once. It distracted her, however, so that it was only at the car that she took it in properly that the man Norman did propose to intrude himself between them, and not just on the journey back, to which she had so much looked forward, but into their home. It was too bad.

'Darling, are you being fair to Mr Norman?' she wondered. It was so unreasonable that another possibility occurred to her. 'Unless, of course, you were going on anyway? To Balinter?'

'Where?' Monty Norman asked, and it was obvious that he did not know the village where they lived nor even the town of Balinter, or how far away they might be; and that, horribly, he did not care. He was ready on the strength of a casual meeting on a train to come with them. Yet he must, surely, have travelled for some purpose. No one travelled without a purpose.

That was inexplicable to her.

2

Her mind refused to accept the reality of the white cloth thrown over the corner of the glass, and as drowsily she questioned its presence she began to recognise the familiar corner of their bedroom and the reflection white in the tilted mirror of the window curtain with the sunlight behind it.

Going to meet Maitland . . . so excited . . . surely it said something about the youthfulness of her heart. What a fool you are! thought some Lucy Inside, and she came fully awake.

Abruptly she rolled over. Maitland's bed was empty. What time was it? They had come home and the afternoon had passed and they had eaten that good dinner – a long leisurely meal with wine – just as she had planned it. But not for three.

—Tomorrow, Maitland had said when at last they were alone, I have to go into the Department, but I'll take him off when I get back. He had turned away from her and gone to sleep.

Perhaps, she thought, Maitland has come back and collected him and gone off again. He might not have wanted to waken her. Perhaps she had slept the morning away. Anyway, even if Maitland's inexplicable guest was still here, why should she be hospitable? Wasn't he the reason she had slept so badly last night? Closing her eyes, she felt the pressure in her bladder, conspiratorial, adding to the luxury of warmth and lying very still. A noise raised her head from the pillow. He might be wandering the house, prying. When she did get up, she had waited too long and had to crouch against the discomfort as she hurried to the door.

She went softly past the bedroom on the upper landing then remembered he had been put for the night into the little room at the back. Its door was closed. With a groan she scuttled into the bathroom. As if he in his turn might be listening, the gush of her water embarrassed her, though there was no controlling the pleasure of its issuing.

Certainly, the house felt empty. After looking in the front room, she peeped into Maitland's study and then the back sitting-room. When there was no one in the big kitchen-dining room at the rear of the house, she relaxed, sure she had the place to herself.

As she drifted about the rooms, she could have placed every item of furniture, every ornament, and told where each one had been bought or by whom gifted. This little chair by the phone, re-covered in velvet to be respectable, had come from their first house and that chiffonier from an auction in Annan (the clearing out of some country mansion, furniture piled in the stalls of the cattle market) and the desk in Maitland's study they'd bought specially for coming here eleven years ago. She stared blindly at the painting that hung behind the desk, not seeing it but the day on which it had been bought . . . Sun in the park and the vivid colours like exotic flowers attracting them so that they ran hand in hand across the lawns to where railings were made over into a summer gallery of student art and the painters, the young painters – but the world was young then – and Maitland smiling at the girl and crying, Yes! though we can't afford it, five pounds, five whole pounds! . . . Laughing, But all the same we're going to have it! we're not going to let this one go – it's beautiful! – it's an investment – we're investing in you, we're investing in your talent! – this is our investment of faith in you. And she had never forgotten the wonderful look which the girl had given him when he said that to her – the look, yes, the look had been beautiful – as for the painting, privately she thought it a drab thing, a little square of brown colours, four potatoes on a cloth – but at some lost level of her mind she had never ceased to be warmed by the event of the girl's response – as if Maitland, not really all that much older and with no power or place in the world, had been able to give a promise, a key to the future, golden like the sun; from somewhere in himself he had given the girl that as with authority. The painting had been the first thing Maitland and she had bought together; the following year they married.

But, of course, hung on a wall always in the same place any painting ceased to be seen. Not for years had she consciously examined it or thought of the girl and her joy in being young, in the miracle of her talent, all the uncertain future ahead of her and the wonder of a stranger's reassurance. He could make that kind of promise and be believed. He was Maitland even then . . .

She could not recall the girl's name. When she came close to the canvas, she could make out the word Beth, but that did not jog her memory, and the name which followed was no more than a squiggle of the brush. But three years later, or it might have been four, after their marriage anyway, Maitland had unexpectedly made up his mind to discover what had become of the artist. She's going to be a success, he had said, just like I told her – this little canvas could be the cornerstone of our fortune. Married? he had been angry when she suggested that. What are you talking about? No, she had dedication that girl, she'll be in an attic somewhere painting, and the word will just be beginning to get out.

He had asked questions in galleries, looked through catalogues and journals, at first almost casually. As he found no one to admit having heard of the girl, however, his will took on a sharper edge until she would have hesitated to raise again the possibility that the girl might be married and have lost interest in being an artist. Yet it did not seem to her impossible; the impulse to create touched many people but for most of them – and not least

17

for women when marriage came – it was no more than a part of being young. She imagined the girl by a fire, holding a baby; why would she not be content?

And at the thought that Maitland, so exuberantly more gifted than anyone else in their circle, might be wrong, just for this once, there was the faintest shameful touch of satisfaction; but even that had changed to an unfamiliar concern as he persisted in his search, writing to friends from his own student days and following up every connection with the world of art. About then, if she had been driven to put into words the vague burden of her anxiety, it would have been an apprehension that Maitland had identified the promise he had made not simply with the girl's future but with his own: perhaps he too had never forgotten the look on the girl's face as if it were a mirror in which he had seen the image of the man he was going to be. Whatever was the truth, she never had to bring that perception to the surface, for finally it had been a friend of the girl who had written to him. Beth is dead, the letter said; she died that summer of the exhibition in the park. Maitland had never spoken of the painting again or paid it any attention. If she had not asked him, he would not even have told her about the letter. If it hadn't been for me, she thought, the painting would be lost now or lying in an attic. It was after all just the same picture whether the girl was dead or alive; just the same picture as the one he had fallen in love with that day in the park. It wasn't the picture's fault that the girl had died.

Going from one room to another, she could name the price of everything, the shop, the auction, by whose gift – and wasn't that natural? Home was the place where what you saw told a story. If all these stories were added together, was that to be the sum of her life? Would there be nothing left over? The trouble with you is that you're too contented, she told herself. It's not good for anyone to be too much . . . too much . . . Her hold of the fancy slackened and it drifted away. Where normally everything pleased her, nothing did. All her familiar pos ssions . . .

18

Like a jail, she thought, standing by the front door with her hands hanging by her sides, like a prison. A prison without any guards or bars. I guard myself. I turn the key.

And with that she came to her senses in fright. I've wakened in a strange mood, she decided, and felt better as if she had diagnosed and prescribed the cure all at once. She was not properly awake. She needed breakfast; with the thought, she was ravenous. With somewhere to go, she hurried. So energetically did she thrust open the kitchen door that it sprang back and struck her on the wrist. Fluffing up eggs yellow in a pan, she felt the burn and nip of the knock and wiped tears from her eyes. Seated at the divider between kitchen and dining area, she ate so greedily that pieces of the scrambled egg sprayed in crumbs from her lips. She was bent forward, dabbing them up so that nothing would escape her hunger, when she glanced to the side and saw a figure on the other side of the glass door.

From the garden, with his face close against the glass, Monty Norman was watching her. As she stumbled to her feet, he opened the door and stepped inside.

'You have a lovely home,' he said, the deep voice so calm, so indifferent to her fright, that she could have imagined for a moment he was making fun of her. 'That view,' he went on, 'all the way across to the mountains. I was standing at the bottom of your garden and they looked close enough to touch. There didn't seem to be anything between me and the snow on top of them. I felt good. As if I'd got the jump on the day being up so early.'

Her glance turned helplessly to the blue-faced clock above the dresser. It read half-past eleven. 'Did you see Maitland – my husband – this morning?'

Uninvited, he sat at the table, though she remained standing. 'He'd gone when I got up. I thought maybe you might have gone with him.'

Did he imagine they would have left him alone in the house?

19

'There's a meeting of his department this morning. It won't be long until he's home.'

'Not long?' he wondered. 'Mid-afternoon – wasn't that what he said? Last night, wasn't that what he said?'

'I left you talking together, Mr Norman. I went to bed early.'

'Monty,' he said. 'You didn't manage it last night, but I thought we'd got beyond Mr Norman. I thought we'd settled for not calling me anything.'

It seemed he had charm; and perhaps it was only her impression that he was conscious of it and calculated its use which prevented her from responding. Still, it would have been easy to smile. To avoid what she felt as a difficulty she busied herself gathering up the plate and knife she had been using.

'Have you eaten yet? Did you get breakfast?'

'I raided the fridge. Not knowing whether you were here or not, I helped myself. I'm a good cook.'

'I'm sure you are.'

'You sound as if you don't approve.'

'Sorry?' She ran the plate under the tap and set it upright in the drying rack.

'You don't like me saying I'm good. You think that's pushy.'

And this time the smile was there despite herself, for the memory that came was pleasant to her. By a kind of reaction, she frowned. 'My grandmother,' she said, 'always told us that empty pots rattled loudest.'

She was not a woman to whom rudeness came easily and she felt her heart beat more rapidly.

'Don't they always think they know best, the old women? My mother was just the same. Maybe a bit more,' he smiled and held up his clenched fist, '*emphatic* than I expect your gran was.'

He could go into the front room to read; if he had no interest in books, he could go for a newspaper or simply for a walk. He had talked about the mountains; let him walk up the Brae Road and he'd see across three counties and as many mountains as the horizon would hold. How else would they pass the endless time until Maitland came home?

But as she tried to put one of these questions into words, he asked, 'Could I change my mind?'

'I'm sorry?'

'And have some coffee. It would be no trouble to make it myself.'

'Oh, no!' But that was excessive, and more mildly she finished, 'You've made your own breakfast already. That's bad enough.'

The water ran through the grounds and flowed down the rod of the Cona. 'Smells good,' he said appreciatively. 'You're going to have some with me?'

There seemed no reason to refuse; and pouring the cups, adding milk, fetching sugar for him, she was drawn into a pattern of domestic routine. She settled opposite him. It might have been any one of those leisurely breakfasts that went with the mornings when Maitland was free.

'If you'd said to me when I got on the train I'd be sitting here – in a place like this – with someone like you – I'd have laughed in your face.' He sighed comfortably. 'Shows you can't read the future, no use trying.'

'You met my husband just by chance then?' His look seemed to her to parody surprise. She cried, 'I know you said you got talking on the train. Only I wondered if – I thought perhaps you might have met before.'

'No, I'm just a stray. This isn't the first time Maitland's brought one of them home, I'm sure.' He took up the pot, offering her more, and on her refusal poured his own. 'He's a remarkable man. And I don't say that just because he's offered me a job.'

Was there something at the University, something in the office? He didn't seem the academic type, nor even educated, not like her idea of a properly educated man – and if that was snobbery it was based on signals from him she could sense but not analyse. Signals though that Maitland for all his cleverness might not pick up, perhaps because

21

he spent so much of his life with students. Could that be it? Could Norman be a student, some kind of mature student? No one had said what he did. It would explain a good deal. Perhaps Maitland had offered him a little work; helping with the research on his book, reading through material in a library, but that wouldn't pay much.

'Late last night, after you'd gone to bed,' he said as if answering a question. 'He wants me to work for the Trust.' She stared at him in disbelief. 'I understood the Professor spent a lot of his time on it . . .' For a moment, his certainty wavered.

'Are you talking about the Gregory and Rintoul?'

'That's right!' He gave it an emphasis of relief.

'What on earth has he promised to you?'

He regarded her thoughtfully. 'I'm going to raise funds for them. We haven't quite settled on a title for what I'll be doing.'

'Mr Norman, the Gregory and Rintoul already has an administrative secretary. A very good one, I believe.'

'Didn't realise it was something you were involved with. I thought it was just an interest of your husband's.'

The first foretaste of nausea came as a premonition – a shimmer on the edge of vision like a shadow passing across a hill slope before the storm breaks. God! she prayed, don't let me be ill. Not now. Not in front of him.

Since nothing mattered now but to be well, she explained softly, in a tone that seemed like indifference, 'Rintoul is my maiden name. The Trust was founded by my grandfather. By him and Charles Gregory. There aren't any of the Gregorys left. Charles Gregory had no children of his own. After his death, his younger brother took over his part in the Trust. And then he had a son who carried it on after a fashion – but they emigrated to Australia, the son and his family I mean, and since then . . .'

The headache had begun or rather its faintest preliminary touch, not anything to fear or dread in itself; only it meant that what was coming was inevitable and that made it cruel and like a mockery.

'I didn't know. He didn't say. Not about you being the Rintoul in Gregory and.'

'I don't take an active part. But Maitland,' she could not resist her pride in that, 'has made all the difference. Things had been allowed to slide. With the Gregorys planning to go abroad – I don't think you make up your mind to something like that overnight ... I'm sure you have it grow on you, and you get gradually less and less involved with things in the country you're preparing yourself to leave. And my father was dead by then – and I was too young – still at University ...' The lights at the corner of her vision slowed and dimmed. Perhaps it was going to be all right. Without any transition, she said abruptly, 'With the best will in the world my husband can't simply offer you a job. There is a Committee which is responsible for the running of the Trust.'

Unexpectedly he grinned. 'From what he said last night that shouldn't be a problem. The Professor gave me the impression they'll do whatever he tells them to do.'

Like a salesman, she thought, but one who is quite sure he has made his sale.

'No,' she said. 'Mrs Stewart is perfectly capable. There's no need. What you describe seems to me quite a new idea.'

With his spoon he took out a little sweet sediment from the bottom of his cup and licked it off. 'I've only met one person called Rintoul in my whole life. It's not a common name. Maybe I should tell you about him some time.'

But now, the deceptive respite over, the cloud was moving, drifting, its shadow pressing back the light. She was going to be ill. The headache would wound and sicken and for a time leave her blind. Before that happened, she had to be on her own. Far away a voice made her excuse. Guided by flickering cracks of vision, she drew herself upwards, clutching the banister like a lifeline. With eyes closed, she groped along the upper landing and reached the shelter of her bedroom. She had to lie down but it would bring her no relief. It was like what they did to prisoners – everywhere now it seemed – kept them awake until they were broken. If someone had planned this for her, it would be a torment like theirs. She could not bear it.

She opened her eyes against the glare at the sound of the bedroom door being opened. He was standing over her.

'I could see you were ill,' he said. 'You don't have to suffer it on your own. I can help. I've helped other people.'

'You're not a doctor.' She wanted him to say, yes, yes, he was.

'You know I'm not.'

She was disappointed, not angry, cruelly disappointed.

'But has any doctor helped you? Haven't you always hoped for help instead of finding it?'

It was true.

In the echoing tilting isolation of her need, she cried, I believe in you.

Help me.

3

It didn't take much to amuse students. She wondered, though, why Maitland felt he had to make a joke at that point. It was like a disclaimer, for she knew that in a certain mood the story could bring tears to his eyes. It had been a long time, that was true, since she had heard him tell it.

'Quite alone in the middle of the night, he wrote to his wife, "My brain burns. I must have *walked* and a fearful dream rises upon me. I cannot bear the horrible thought. God and Father of the Lord Jesus Christ, have mercy upon me".'

Sophie, had that been her first name? She scanned the lines of heads bent before her, the occasional glimpse of a profile. The girl in the front row – But she turned to smile at her neighbour, appreciating something Maitland had just said, the little chuckle going back wave on wave, ah, they appreciated, all of them appreciated him – and, no, it wasn't Miss Lindgren. Sophie . . .

When she came out, Sam Wilson was lurking. '*Such* devotion!' he cried. 'Quite beyond the *call* of duty!'

Little Sam as Maitland called him, which was unkind, but it was possible not to feel in the mood for yet another of his jokes about her habit of slipping in to sit on one of the back benches if she had to wait for Maitland. Why should he care, why should it be anyone's business, that she still enjoyed listening to her husband lecture?

*

On the fringe of the loch there was a skin of ice.

'Should I feel guilty?' she asked.

'He'll have gathered ammunition and some of it will be useful, but I can manage just as well without it.'

'All the same, if you promised to go over his paper for the Dean's meeting . . .'

'Don't worry. It's too fine an afternoon to spend indoors listening to Sam. Anyway all the horse trading has been done, the cuts decided. He doesn't understand the politics of this place.'

'I was rude to him. I can cope usually. It's just that today . . .' She sighed. 'He's devoted to you. I should like him for that. I do like him. It's just that I don't see why it should make him jealous of everybody, including me.'

'He's actually fond of you, give him half a chance. There's a streak of chivalry in little Sam.'

'You treat him badly.'

'Not a bit of it.' Maitland was surprised. 'He enjoys making drafts. Getting the facts marshalled. Academics love that; like holding meetings. "On a point of order, Vice Chancellor." It gives them – us, me – the illusion of controlling events.'

'Illusion?' She shivered. 'I hadn't realised it was so cold. Take my hand – feel how cold it is.' From the top of the bank she caught glints of late afternoon sun coming up from the ice. 'I'm getting old.'

'Rubbish!' he said.

'Ice, already. Sign of a hard winter. Like all the berries on the rowans or when the starlings leave.'

He laughed and they began to walk again, turning back in the direction that would take them to the car-park.

Under the clear water near the edge she could see smooth round pebbles that emerging made a little patch of shore. On the other side of the loch, the low white buildings of the administrative block and residences were set like toys at the foot of dark soggy-looking hills. The site was beautiful but she had always been bothered by the notion that the University's buildings were temporary and out of place. Perhaps because they were functional in style and of concrete they could only seem like afterthoughts in this dark landscape.

'Country lore,' Maitland said.

'What?'

'Rowans and starlings. But the ice has more to do with the hills keeping the sun away most of the day. You get ice on that stretch in August.'

She smiled at the slyness of his pleasure. He was a connoisseur of her credulity and would sometimes test its limits as if she might believe the most outrageous thing if he assured her it was so.

'That sounds like our summers,' she said.

He bent and picked up a stone from the edge of the path. With a swing and jerk of his arm he sent it curving out, and watched frowning as it punched through the skim ice.

'When I was fourteen,' he said, rubbing his fingers clean, 'there was a winter like that one we had five years back. There was a lochan in the hills above our village. I climbed up to it late one afternoon, and it was frozen from side to side. I'll bet I could walk across, I said to myself.'

'Were you alone?'

'The lochan was about a mile long – very narrow – perhaps two hundred yards across where I was standing. Above on the headland there was a lighthouse. The lochan had been made in the old days by the lighthouse people to give them fresh water. Across on the other side, directly opposite me, was a pump house. That was my mark. I was about halfway before I started to get worried. I heard the ice crack and felt it bending under me.'

'Don't tell me,' she said. 'I don't want to hear.'

'On the other side I could see the trees without any leaves, just little trails of mist winding through the branches. It was the cold in my legs got me moving again. As I got near, I could see the grass bent over under the ice on the bank. If I'd gone through, the current would have carried me down to the dam across the landward end. I'd have got trapped there and stayed until the thaw came. Unless, of course, someone had looked down and seen me staring through the ice at them with a face as yellow as the grass.'

But she refused to be horrified. 'Funny you've never told me that before. It's the kind of story you like to tell.'

'Every man his own hero.'

He unlocked the car doors and she watched through the window as they passed the staff club and more residences and then were on the road that would take them through the town and put them on the way for home.

—Dearest Lydia, she remembered it had gone, dearest children, farewell. My brain burns as the recollection grows. My dear, dear wife, farewell. Hugh Miller.

Born Comarty 1802, the son of a middle-aged ship's master and an eighteen-year-old mother, Harriet Wright. Died on Christmas Eve 1856. They had found him with a bullet in his chest and the revolver in his hand. In between he made himself a scientist who impressed Darwin, a writer admired by Dickens.

'You made a joke of his signing his name in full. You never used to.'

With the telepathy of the long-married, he answered, 'On a note like that. Telling her of his suicide.' It didn't take long to get through Balinter; they were on to a country road again. ' "Hugh Miller." Sometimes those old Victorians seem like aliens from another planet.'

'But it didn't mean he didn't love her. Wasn't that the point? That behind the changes of language the feelings stay the same?'

'Hmmm,' he said.

'All right, I understand,' she persisted, 'that it's about paradigms. About Lamarck and Darwinism coming and Miller not being able to bear it. And his "elevatory fiats" and how the Creationists have to follow just the same line because their belief system doesn't give them any choice. And how Marxist scientists take the discontinuities and get quite keen on them for *their* own reasons – making

28

nature advance in bursts of revolutionary change. What was it you said? – "It gathers all of prehistory for them into the neat paradigm of the dialectic." I know all that. But all the same . . .'

'I married you because you were my prettiest student,' he said.

'Not the cleverest.'

'At the end of my first year's stint as a lecturer, pretty was what counted.' There was silence for a while, and when she stole a glance at him he was frowning so that she expected him to make some grumble about the flat spread of the familiar landscape. Instead, he said, 'I found him a place to stay in Edinburgh.'

'Who?'

'Monty Norman. It'll be convenient if he goes to work with the Trust.' Round the long curve of the road, she could see the hill that rose into their village. 'I thought I might put it to the Committee next week.' They began the sharp brief ascent. 'Do you mind?'

'No.'

As they came level with the inn, he braked and swung the car across the road into their drive. 'I don't know,' he said. He switched off the engine and the silence buzzed. 'I don't know, it's only an idea. Nothing settled.'

'Put it to the Committee.'

'I don't know . . .'

'I want you to,' she heard herself saying. 'I *want* you to.'

Inside he found her sitting at the table in the kitchen, hand shading her eyes from the light.

'I'm sorry,' he said. 'I didn't realise.' He rubbed gently at the nape of her neck.

'It's just that if you promised . . .'

'Rest for a bit. I'll help you upstairs in a little while.' His thumbs pressed and stroked, again, again. '. . . I'll probably go through with it . . . The Norman thing . . . See what happens . . .'

She felt better.

'Like a duckling,' she said, her voice muffled as her head hung forward.

'Sorry?'

'Sam Wilson. That winter five years ago on the University loch. Skating behind you like a duckling following the mother duck.'

'Everyone waiting to see if it would bear our weight. All that space to ourselves. It was like flying.'

'I expected every moment to see you vanish through the ice.'

'You should have come. I would have supported you.'

He glowed for her again in memory sliding against the keen rapture of the wind.

'. . . Perhaps if we'd been on our own. But with all those students there – I didn't want to collapse in front of them all, let you down. Perhaps if it freezes again this year, I'll try. Shall I? It could happen this year with ice there already – we should check on the rowan berries. And the starlings.'

'No,' he said, so softly she turned her head a little to hear, 'that winter won't come back again. You have to take it while it's there.'

4

The stairs curved up out of sight. There was a door facing her and another in the corner, but she knew that Julian Chambers would come down from above to greet her and lead her up to the first floor where he preferred to have his room. There were magazines on the low table, but she was passing the time by listening.

'There is the other possibility,' the woman was saying to the girl at the desk. She was neatly dressed in a black coat which had been expensive when it was bought a little too long ago. 'They open my letters. You see the implication? It's the other possibility for the money, isn't it?'

'I've explained Mr Thomson isn't available this morning.' Pulling a face of wry irritation, the girl glanced at Lucy, who refused the conspiracy. The woman was a client of the firm. It was really too bad. She was sure Julian Chambers would not approve of the woman being slighted in this way.

'Mr Thomson,' she lowered her voice cunningly, 'has to be told. In case anything happens to me. But I couldn't tell you, it wouldn't be safe.'

'There's no chance of seeing Mr Thomson,' the girl said. 'Mr Byers could have a word with you.'

As if on cue, the door in the corner opened and a plump smooth young man in a three-piece suit came out, crying as he came, 'Now then, Mrs Willis. If you come with me, we can chat about whatever's upsetting you.'

'It's wicked of them. It's not possible for me to live on

what's coming in. It was never like this when Jim was alive.'

'Ah, well, let's you and I go over things. I'm sure we can set your mind at rest.' His tone was kindly and patient and very satisfied with its patience and content with its kindness. Before he whisked her inside, he did not resist the glance about him of an actor in search of applause.

'She's been in already this morning,' the girl at the desk said. 'I warned them somebody would have to deal with her. I can't be expected to do it on my own. I have work to do, too.'

'It seems very sad,' Lucy said. 'I suppose it isn't possible that there is something wrong with her money?'

The girl shook her head dismissively. 'There may not be enough of it. We all have that problem. Her husband's dead and she imagines things.'

'It must be hard to be so lonely.'

'Lonely,' the girl repeated, weighing the word like an amateur diagnosis.

Mad then, Lucy thought. I don't suppose being even a little mad is easier. Unless, of course, you were a happy maniac. I believe that's possible. I wonder if mad and happy is preferable to sane and wretched. That poor woman – not very sane and really rather wretched.

As she pondered that, Julian Chambers reached over the banisters and began his apologies, which went on until he arrived before her.

'So busy – and just at the wrong moment. I hadn't expected you, of course. If I had known . . . Not too interminable a wait, however? It's splendid to see you – after such a time, and looking so well.' He climbed the stairs ahead of her, his lean old haunches pumping him upwards with the energy of a schoolboy. 'It must be, two years, is it, surely not three?'

He stood aside and going into the familiar room she took the comfortable chair by the table rather than one of the clients' chairs set before his desk.

'Oh, I think so,' she said. 'Quite as long as that.'

'Maitland keeps me in touch, of course.' He settled himself behind the desk, folding his long frame almost out of sight. 'I ask for you.'

'You look the same to me,' she said. 'You never change.'

'I fancy I've done so since our first meeting. You were chuckling in your mother's arms, and were quite charming in a christening robe. That would be almost – it wouldn't be right, would it, to say how many years? It would be ungallant. Or is that old-fashioned? At seventy-three, I feel I can allow myself to be.'

'No one would believe it. Sixty perhaps.'

'No,' he said firmly. He had sunk down so that she, taught in childhood to sit up straight, looked down on the white clean curve of his brow. 'That's flattering but not so. I look like what I am – a well preserved seventy-year-old who's blessed with good health and fortunate enough to be one of the lucky few who don't have to comply with any nonsense about retiring. I shan't retire. I'll go on like this and one day someone like you will say, You might be sixty – and the next the deception will cease and some unconsidered piece of the machinery wear out and I shall be dead.'

He paused as if there was a response she might care to enter at this point, but since what he had said was truth so clearly expressed it did not occur to her to offer any comfort. She waited with hands passive in her lap and as though pumped under pressure he rose up until he had straightened himself behind the shelter of the desk.

'I wondered,' she said diffidently, 'if there would be any problem about my attending the Trust meeting next Wednesday.'

He stared blankly, looking his age in that mild confusion, until recovering he said, 'A place for you is there at any of our meetings. Of right, as it were.' He reflected. 'Is Maitland unwell? If there is some point he wishes to be covered, I could present it. There wouldn't be any need for you to trouble yourself.'

'He'll be there. It's just that I'd like to be there too.'

At a loss, he frowned. 'Then there's something that . . .' A shadow of irritability clouded his gallantry.

'When I think of my father,' she said, 'I feel I should have been more involved. But Maitland was there and I felt I would hardly be missed – not while Maitland was there.'

'You say he'll be there on Wednesday. He's well enough? Yes . . . But you'd like to be present also.'

'My father put so much of himself into the Trust.'

It was all she had to offer, and his acceptance of it as some kind of explanation would allow her also to be satisfied. 'As of right'; she had a right to be there; that's what he had said.

'Your father would have been older than I, if he had been spared. I find that strange. When I think of him, I think of a young man – so filled with energy and purpose.' He sighed. 'The war killed him though he survived it. As it did so many others – so many of those who died in the nineteen fifties. They should have put Killed In Action on their graves. It would have been more honest. All part of the price this country paid.'

She remembered his wife was dead, but found she had no memory of his children, whether he had any or what had become of them. 'The Trust owes so much to you.'

'It went down after your father's death – even before Gregory went off to Australia. I did my best for your father's sake, but I was working hard to build up the practice in those years. I hardly ever saw Emily or the girls. It seemed the right thing to do, at the time.' He paused, and then began again as if remembering what he had intended to say. 'Maitland's made the difference.' He directed a fresh look of speculation upon her. 'You'll find our meetings are very much a matter of routine. There isn't anything coming up of particular interest.'

'It's a matter of . . . staffing,' she said. Of course, that was why.

The old man jerked his hand up as if to constrain her to silence. A touch of red dabbed each cheek. 'Oh, dear,' he said. 'The Trust still has a role to play. There's plenty for it still to do.'

She was perplexed. 'Of course, there is.'

'That's why there mustn't be any breath of scandal.'

'Scandal?'

'I can't believe,' Julian Chambers leaned forward, bent the height of his age to her, 'that there could be any satisfaction in the longer term, however real the injury. Another way of dealing with things? And, in any case, there's more to be said for salvaging than destroying, and that's an opinion derived from a lifetime of witnessing such matters. A relationship has so much of value that is lost sight of in the heat of the moment. Concentrate on what is of value, however real the injury. However real the injury.'

The dry passion of his tone rose and ceased.

'I'm terribly sorry,' Lucy said.

For what? This stupid compulsion to apologise; laughter tickled her and escaped. At the expression on the old man's face, disgracefully it increased. 'I'm sorry,' she gasped. 'I really am so dreadfully sorry.'

'Now!' he warned and rose from his seat.

Dimly she apprehended the notion that his code of the necessary might accommodate a slap to the cheek of an hysterical woman. For his sake more than her own, she struggled for control, afraid that the slap administered would tax him beyond the bounds of their long acquaintance.

'I can't imagine what's wrong with me,' she managed and hiccuped. 'It's just that I don't know what you're talking about.'

'There was never any intention of forcing a confidence,' he said and, to her further surprise, as if she had offended him.

'But it's all right. I mean if there's anything I can tell you about Mr Norman. If you feel it might help you to decide,' she said.

'Decide? Decide what, what is there to decide?'

'About the post with the Trust. I met him, you see. He stayed with us.'

'He's to be offered a post? Mr Norman, is that the name?'

'But I assumed you knew.'

'Not a word. And this is why – only this – nothing else?'

He pulled at his lip. She remembered that with him as a gesture of doubt. What on earth was there in what she had said to disbelieve? The unwanted laughter stirred, and as she pressed her lips together holding it in, she saw his expression alter as he watched her.

Ridiculous even only for a moment to feel surrounded by mysteries. Ridiculous to feel afraid.

Yet it did seem, if only for a moment, as if for nothing more than the accident of a moment's laughter, that this old dry man might hate her.

5

On the Monday morning, two days before the Trust
meeting was due, restless and out of sorts she took herself
into Balinter for lunch. She hesitated outside the restaurant
Maitland usually took her to and then wandered on until
almost out of the small town centre she found a wine bar
that was new to her. She began to eat, a pizza with half a
pint of light lager to go with it, and then found she had no
appetite. A sign pointed her down a flight of steps. There
was a telephone booth, the standard street model of an
earlier time but painted blue, set up solid and improbable
outside the ladies' lavatory. It seemed to her like an item
of camp decoration and she was surprised when a tug
opened the door. The little mirror inside distorted her face
in its coarse grain. The phone was still there and a coin
box, and when she took up the receiver the waiting note
of an open line buzzed in her ear. She could not think of
anyone to phone and put the receiver back down, feeling
silly and glad there was no one to see her. The squares of
glass divided outside into framed segments of emptiness
trying to make up a room: a table with an unlit candle
stuck in the neck of a bottle, blue red yellow squashed
together in gaudy prints, the bottom steps of the flight that
went up to the ground floor. She avoided the eyes of the
face in the mirror. The Tardis was a police box not a
telephone box and it shimmered and vanished and that
meant it had flown off with you into some other part of
the universe. Inside this box it was quiet. She listened to

her breath and wondered, if the phone rang, would she pick it up?

The train jolted to a halt, clanked forward and settled to rest. Isolated flakes of snow swam past the windows. Across the tracks a black dog was chasing its tail. It chased it into a yard, spinning and lunging one way and then the other. The train began to move; she turned her head straining to keep the dog in view until the last possible moment. It rippled like a stick along a fence, the iron strokes of railings herding it back out of her sight into the past.

Maitland would not be home for dinner: a meeting, something; as so often lately, he would be dining out. A train to the city, then, why shouldn't she? Afterwards a train back to Balinter and catch the last bus.

In Edinburgh a lid of clouds pressed down on the roofs and the wind chilled and hurried her along. She studied the bright dressed spaces of store windows, but felt no desire to go inside. The pedestrian precinct in the lane above Princes Street was swept almost bare of life, although it was only early afternoon. The wind raked along its length and blew a man like a pencil smudge from one side to the other and erased him in a doorway. In the window of a travel agent, sand and blue sea, a brown girl stretching up to catch the sun; she was at the entry which led up to the offices of the Gregory and Rintoul Trust. She stared at the brass plate, seeing the name as if for the first time.

The staircase had been painted yellow, which came as a surprise. On the first floor there was an insurance office. Had that been here before? On the second two blank closed doors. She went more slowly, confidence ebbing as she climbed.

There was a passage beyond the Trust entrance with a toilet and a storeroom and then round the corner a short corridor with three more doors behind which were the offices proper. The whole suite had been gifted just after the war by a friend of her father's, a businessman whose son had died in the fighting round Cannes. For a time, money left by him had met the rates and gone to defray the annual phone bill; more than anything, the gift had kept the Trust going in its worst years. Now everyone spoke of inflation. Her thoughts touched lightly upon Monty Norman – someone who would raise money – wasn't that so?

She opened the first door, but instead of being Mrs Stewart's office it was a larger room with an oval table occupying the middle of the floor. Bundles of folders were lined up in neat rows on top of it. In the passage again, the remaining doors were of plain wood and unglassed. A plate was screwed to the upper panel of the second, however, a little thing easy to miss: 'M. E. Stewart, Administrative Secretary', and now from inside came the unexpected sound of laughter. As she stretched out her hand, the door opened away from her, a young woman swung out, broke step, and was past and off.

'Can I help you?' It was a tall older woman with pale fine-drawn features, rising from behind a desk. 'This is the Gregory and Rintoul Trust. Have you been in touch with us? . . . You are in the right place?'

'It's Mrs Stewart, isn't it?' Having found her voice, Lucy was relieved by its firmness. 'I'm Professor Ure's wife.'

How else should she describe herself?

'How awful of me! Now, to be fair, it has been *such* a long time.' With a shepherding gesture, she gathered Lucy into the office and called out into the corridor, 'Sophie, be a dear, would you? Make coffee and bring it through. Would you do that, please?'

Sophie?

Settled again behind her desk, Mrs Stewart summoned a look of enquiry. As the silence lengthened, Lucy felt her face crumple into a smile. Mrs Stewart responded and then returned to being puzzled. They avoided one another's eye. At last the girl appeared with the coffees carried on a tin tray with a motif of pink flowers. It was odd, Lucy thought, the things that caught one's attention.

'I'm afraid they've both been milked – is that all right? Sure? She could fetch another.'

The girl had hesitated, perhaps expecting to be introduced, but now as the cup was finally handed over Lucy heard the door click shut behind her.

'Sugar, then?'

'My husband nagged me until I stopped.'

'I can imagine,' Mrs Stewart said, 'that it would be difficult to refuse the Professor once he had set his heart on something.'

'Oh, it was quite long ago,' Lucy said vaguely.

Mrs Stewart became busy setting the tray to one side. 'None of us take sugar, you see, and so when we have a visitor that's when sometimes we find we're out, completely out. Oh, but biscuits? We certainly have those!'

Lucy shook her head. 'I was passing. I shouldn't be keeping you from your work.'

'We have a break about now. In the afternoon. We get through the work all the same.'

God! Lucy thought, I'm not criticising. By a kind of reflex, she wondered how efficient Mrs Stewart was.

'I'm coming to the meeting on Wednesday, you see. And so I thought I would look in. Find my way, after such a long time.'

'But Professor Ure will be coming?'

She had heard that note in too many other voices to mistake it. She added Mrs Stewart to the number of Maitland's devotees.

'Oh, it's not that he won't be there.'

'But there's something which interests you?'

Julian Chambers had asked the same question. As for rights, who had more right than she to be at a meeting of the Trust? She was the last surviving Rintoul. Whatever her reason, she had the right.

'Perhaps there's an agenda you could let me have?'

'Professor Ure will have received one. They go out to let the Committee prepare.'

'For myself. I'd like one for myself.'

'Of course.'

Lucy tried to take in the detail of the items. None of it meant much to her. There was no mention of Monty Norman or the plan to create a new appointment.

'The yellow sheet is the agenda. The blue ones give background information on matters that will come up. We've found that helpful. The minutes of the previous meeting are on the white sheets. The paragraphs are numbered for ease of reference.'

'I'll read it – read them all.'

'I can give you the minutes of the meeting before the last one. Would you want those?'

'No – please.'

Mrs Stewart who had sketched an intention of getting up again settled back. 'The Professor has them all, of course. If there was anything.'

'I shouldn't have time. These will keep me busy.'

They sipped coffee and made some kind of conversation. When there was no more to say, or rather when the effort to fill that lack became too great, they ended it. Mrs Stewart walked her to the head of the stairs.

Halfway down the flight, Lucy turned back. In the corridor of the Trust suite, she listened at the secretary's door for voices or laughter. There was the sound of a phone ringing and stopping almost at once as if it had been lifted. With a light hasty step, she went back to the first door and not giving herself time to think opened it and went inside.

The girl was tidying the bundles of papers set out on the long table. She did not seem surprised to see Lucy.

'Is it in here the meeting is to be held? Of the Committee, I mean.'

The girl cross-hatched one bundle on to another. 'Yes. But all of this stuff will be cleared away by then.'

'We'll sit at this table . . .' The girl didn't say anything, perhaps since the answer was obvious. 'Are there enough chairs?'

'We bring them in from next door,' the girl said, smiling as if the question amused her. Methodically she went on arranging the bundles.

'I'm interrupting.'

'This is the old leaflet – telling about the work the Trust does. Soon, though, we're going to have a campaign to coincide with Christmas. They haven't – *we* haven't done it before but it seems worth trying. Get in touch with social clubs in factories and offices, places like that. Part of the difficulty will be in getting them targeted – to the right people that is. I've been phoning a sample finding which person would be most likely to help.' She said all this pleasantly but with her attention on what she was doing, politely abstracted, terribly busy. Now she laughed. 'Luckily part of the phone bill gets paid for us. Just as well!'

It seemed strange to Lucy that this girl should be explaining the work of the Trust to her. 'My grandfather – I mean, my father – it was his friend . . .' She trailed off.

'I know. Rintoul. I mean, that's you, isn't it?'

No, Lucy wanted to say, not just Rintoul. Ure. I'm Professor Ure's wife. But that might have made the girl smile again. Instead, she asked, 'Have you worked here for very long?'

'Not really.'

'You speak so knowledgeably.'

'I'm an enthusiast,' the girl said.

'It's Miss Lindgren, isn't it? You are Miss Lindgren?'

Her own question took her by surprise. She had not intended to ask.

'I didn't like to remind you,' Miss Lindgren said. 'We met at the station. Professor Ure introduced us.'

'My husband.'

'Yes.'

'I had no idea you were with the Trust. Didn't you say you were a student? It's not vacation time.' Premonitions of pain stirred in her head and she touched her hand to the place, and then realising what she was doing snatched it away as if it was a confession of weakness. The girl watched her interestedly. 'Sorting out letters. Surely this can't be much of a job. Couldn't you find something better?'

'The thing is, I identify,' Sophie Lindgren said. 'I really like to get involved. I couldn't bear a job that was just a job.'

Outside, the grey afternoon dazzled her with its light. She stumbled blindly forward until a hard edge of concrete struck her across the thighs. Leaning for support, she ground her knuckles against her forehead. The warning signs told her that soon she would be in pain. The pain would come. Beer cans and cigarette packets littered the frozen earth in the concrete tub, and a shrub shook its sticks in the icy wind. If the lid of the sky rolled back hands would reach down for her. Fingers like claws, probes, levers to open—

A face like wet grey cloth pressed itself almost into hers. All curiosity over a mouth gathered in the ugliness of contempt, it reduced her to one of the women who were despised for blabbering their memories and fears to the indifferent street. Then she saw there were other watchers, three walking youths, the wind pulling at their hair and thin jackets, watching her while she gaped at the blank sky, possessing her with their eyes, her weakness, her folly.

As if he had come out of a poster of the sun, the man stepped from the doorway beside the travel agents.

'It's my impression you were supposed to be here before this,' he said. 'It's all right though. I can see you're not well. We'll go back to my place.'

The dry branches rattled and she was more afraid than ever, until she remembered a voice promising her that nothing was certain.

Not even the coming of pain.

6

Rain during the night had removed the last of the snow from the fields and on the Wednesday morning the sky was as high and blue and shiny as if it had been polished for the occasion.

'You are actually coming,' Maitland said. 'Not that you haven't a perfect right to—'

Perhaps she had taken so little to do with the work of the Committee because her entitlement had nothing to do with what she could bring to it, but only with being her father's daughter. The mild ironical thought occurred to her that if men had the same scruple half the boardrooms in the country would be empty. But, of course, there had been Maitland; so, anyway, she had not been needed.

She was surprised by the outskirts of the city.

'Are you driving too fast?'

'I always drive fast.' He raised an eyebrow. It was unlike her to question what he did.

'It's just,' she tried to bring the idea into focus, 'just that I wondered if you haven't begun to drive more quickly. I've felt that recently without realising it.'

'No,' he said. 'I shouldn't think so.'

'Do you remember Jenny Craigie?' she asked on impulse.

'Should I?'

'She was my friend when I first met you. A stout girl, but always smiling – really rather a pretty face. She used to complain, Oh, not pheasant again! whenever she got a parcel sent her from home. Her father was a gamekeeper, you see, not rich or anything. Usually, in fact, she was short of money. That's what made it so funny – Oh, not pheasant again!'

'And I met her?'

'Oh, yes. She went abroad though, just after we graduated. Somewhere extraordinary like Iceland. I wrote to her but never had a reply.'

He laughed on a note of exasperation. 'Why are we talking about her then?'

'I suppose she wasn't a keeping in touch sort of person . . . I was thinking about what you said the other day. And I remembered Jenny saying, Your Maitland should have been a pirate.'

'Silly thing to say.' But she smiled when, after a moment, he murmured, 'Funny I don't remember her. She sounds a bit of a character.'

'I knew some interesting people. She wasn't your type.'

'Oh, type . . . What was it I said the other day?'

'You said, All the fun's gone since the Garden Noamsky dug his own grave – and that's the deep grammar of *that*!'

And spread out his arms pushing with the palms of his hands as if the hills round the campus were crowding in on him. Standing there by the edge of the frozen loch.

She saw that he was smiling across at her. 'I think it sounded funnier when I said it.' And in the voice of an Irish comedian, 'It's the way you tell them!'

'It didn't sound funny to me. It sounded as if you felt you had made a mistake. And I couldn't understand why. You've made such a success of your life.'

'Sam Wilson with my life – or Marshall or Turner – for them my life would be a success. It isn't good enough for me.'

She was accustomed to the restless flow of his talk and to its touches of excess. He let the silence run on, however, and she thought about what he had said and found she disliked it. She really disliked it a great deal.

'I don't think I've ever heard you being so . . .' she searched and could only find, 'humourless.' As soon as she

45

had used the word, she regretted it. If he had been angered, she would not have been able to defend using it.

After a silence, he said, 'You shouldn't take things I say casually so seriously.'

'You sounded serious,' she said, concentrating on the flow of shopfronts as they left Haymarket behind.

'Perhaps I was irritated because they don't give out Nobel prizes for linguistics. All those molecular biologists are hogging them.'

After all it was she who had been humourless. Her attention was diverted by a change in their route. Instead of going along Princes Street, he had swung right and was beating successive traffic lights on the amber speeding up Lothian Road. 'Didn't I say? We're picking up Monty Norman.'

Just into a street of shabby brownstone tenements, he reversed into a space in a line of parked cars.

'Come up with me to fetch him,' he said. 'There's no point in getting chilled sitting here.'

As they walked along looking for the number, he mused, 'This would have been a fashionable area once, before the First World War perhaps. Now it's all sub-lets, students and multi-occupation. Give it a year or two and the students will be few and far between, the way things are going. There are development plans in the offing too, I believe. We should buy one, Lucy. Rent it out. The place will be sandblasted back into fashion and we'll clear thirty thousand.'

Her husband did not impress her when he talked of ways of making money, not out of any moral objection but because as a girl she had met enough men who had made a great deal to know that Maitland lacked the gift. She did not think less of him for it. The men who possessed it had not been over-endowed with any others as far as she could see. The common factor had been how much making money had mattered to them. None of them would have wasted time on an irrelevancy like the Nobel Prize.

Because the building hadn't been refurbished, the close

had no entryphone, and that meant it smelt of cats and perhaps something worse. As a student she had visited friends in places like this. Then it had seemed like an adventure; now she wished she had stayed in the car.

On the door there was a card pinned at each corner and listing five names in uneven type. The first thing she saw was Monty Norman's name printed at the foot of the list clumsily with a red pen, then that the last of the names typed above it was S. Lindgren. As she registered the name, Norman was opening the door and there was no time to say anything and they were going in and she saw how large the flat was. There were three doors on each side of the corridor before it turned out of sight. Just inside the entrance there was a table with a phone and a full ashtray laid on the book. Her thoughts moved hastily, like insects rowing above the dark stretched surface of a pond. Seeing the cigarette stubs, she placed their dry taint and felt how wretched it would be to live in a place where the air was spoiled by strangers.

The second room on the right, into which Norman led them, had a bed still unmade, a wardrobe and a chair by the window. Someone had hung a calendar turned to a print of an Italian townscape. She noticed it was for the wrong month. The vivid off-shade colours made the room more drab by contrast.

'I decided it would be a good idea if you came with us,' Maitland said.

Monty Norman threw the coverlet in an untidy sprawl across the bed. 'Would that be all right?' To Lucy it was plain he was flustered and angry, but Maitland seemed to catch no hint of that.

'Not into the meeting itself, naturally. You'll wait in Mrs Stewart's room while it's going on. You can bring a book,' he glanced around, 'or a paper, something to pass the time.'

'Would I do any good being there?'

'We'll get it settled today. By tomorrow you'll be working for the Trust. They may agree without seeing you. As a group they're quite biddable. The one who might raise a difficulty is Henney Low, one of Her Majesty's Inspectors of Schools. He'll put up an argument to show how sharp he is, but he'll give in at last because he doesn't really care. On committees, it's the dullard with principles I don't want as an opponent.'

'I wasn't expecting – I'd need to get changed.' Although Norman smiled, Lucy knew how little he was enjoying any of this.

'Fine. My wife will wait outside. But you'll have to make it quick.'

She wandered round the corner and found the kitchen. A frying pan with a lining of white grease lay beside a pile of unwashed dishes; and, though she tried to tighten it, the tap wouldn't stop dripping into the sink. In the corridor, the flat was held in mid-morning stillness apart from the murmur of Maitland's voice. Obviously it was empty. She took hold of the handle of the nearest door. Fractionally slowly, she began to turn it; so intent upon making no noise that her tongue crept out from the corner of her lips as it had done when she was a child.

A man lay on a bed with his hands behind his head staring at her. The room was full of paintings, standing against the walls and leaning on the furniture and propped up on the solitary chair like an easel; the odd thing was that none of them were hung, and she looked back and forward and from side to side at them and the man said nothing, watching her, and she drew the door shut just as quietly as before.

Then her heart began to shake her with its beating and she fled on tiptoe, and would have hidden but couldn't go into the room for Norman was still dressing. She leaned against the wall, trembling, panting for breath, pressing the tips of her fingers hard into her temples, waiting for the man to come into the corridor while behind her through the crack of the door Maitland's voice flowed on.

'Henney Low would make a splendid chairman for a *prorabotka*. That's a Russian word for a very Stalinist practice. They stood some poor devil up to have his faults exposed and criticised by a series of colleagues and quondam friends. None of them, of course, with any real choice if word had come down from on high, say from the Provincial Committee of the Party. It could happen to factory managers or office clerks. Or University professors – I could imagine Henney chairing one of those, mauling some potential rival who'd made the mistake of having a thought of his own. Henney's a born *apparatchik*.'

'I see.'

'*Prorabotka* – comes from the verb *rabotat*, to work. But when you add the *pro* on in front it changes into something like to give someone a going over. Like the *pro* in *propustit* when it's used in the phrase "to put through the mincer".'

'I didn't know that,' she heard Norman's voice saying.

There was a pause and then the sound of Maitland's laughter.

In the car, Maitland asked, 'How do you find your room? Comfortable enough?' And went on without waiting for an answer, 'It isn't ideal, but it is a berth for the moment.'

'I take my comforts where I find them,' Norman said from the passenger seat behind her.

'It's a base,' Maitland said. 'Lucky I heard about it. How are you getting on with your neighbours? Like I said,' he expalined to Lucy, 'all these places are in multiple occupation.'

'It was a help knowing Miss Lindgren,' Norman said.

'She works for the Trust.' Lucy understood Maitland was explaining again for her benefit. 'That's how I heard there was a room coming vacant.'

Lucy nodded but could not find anything to say. She watched the crowds hurrying in and out of the shops.

'You met her,' he persisted, 'you told me you met her when you went to the office on Monday.'

'No,' Lucy said, 'I didn't tell you.'

'Suddenly,' Maitland said, glancing back over his

shoulder, 'my wife has decided to take an interest in the Trust. So that gives you two votes.'

Not that her vote made any difference. Julian Chambers, who had spent an hour on the phone to Maitland the previous evening, took it upon himself to explain the need for a new appointment to co-ordinate and initiate fund raising by the Trust. He reminded the committee of the problems caused by inflation and turned his thoughts back to the nineteen fifties when income from their holdings in tenemental properties had declined almost to nothing. 'For a period, the rights of tenants were so well protected that the needs of owners were lost sight of. It was a time to sell, but . . . a lack of foresight . . . there were difficulties.'

The half-dozen who had put in an appearance for this routine business meeting, barely enough to make them quorate, sank in their seats as the old man worked his way into the Sixties. Lucy sensed Maitland's satisfaction as the pencils doodled. He had amused her with mimicries of Julian prefacing discussions with an historical survey; any potential opposition tended to be numbed into acquiescence.

Even Henney Low's doubts took their foreseen course.

'Last year's muddle over the student fellowship did the Trust's image no good,' Maitland reminded him. 'It wouldn't have happened if May hadn't been off ill, of course,' Mrs Stewart raised her head from the minutes in acknowledgement, 'but it does suggest a need which it's time we met.'

'Even so . . . What quality of person are we likely to get for what we can afford to pay?'

Not only Henney Low was upset when it transpired the discussion was to be supplied with a candidate for the post – only one – and that he was waiting outside. None of them, however, when it came to a decision was obdurate enough to refuse. The Trust was one among many interests. They were busy men. It was that time of the afternoon when everyone was hungry and looking forward to dinner.

50

When Monty Norman came into the room for the second time, it was to be told the decision had been made.

Everything was working out well for him. Without effort, it seemed, he had been provided with a job. Why was it then, Lucy wondered, that he was so full of anger against Maitland? She knew that was so, even if for some reason no one else saw it and even though she could not have explained how she knew.

7

On the Friday morning, she was enormously, inexplicably weary. Even to lift the coffee cup to her lips was an effort. She sat at the table in the kitchen watching the heavy clouds sink down and shroud the mountain summits. The muscles of her sides ached and her legs were heavy. It was as if she had been worked unendurably hard, and there was no reason for it. On impulse it was true she had gone into Edinburgh the day before, and that made her third visit of the week. Once there, though, she had done nothing but wander around and come home again.

Such a waste of time; she wasn't the kind of person who filled the empty days by running off to town, that was trivial. Three times in a week. What was the matter with her? It was ridiculous to be so tired. She stretched her neck and sighed. It was the life she led. She was living the life of an old woman.

Listlessly she contemplated visiting Janet. There was a time when that would have been part of her routine, but it had been weeks since they had spoken. You couldn't count an exchange in the shop or a greeting called from a car. Then there had been the affair of the Sinclairs' party a month ago, after which a week had passed before her reappearance on the village street wearing dark glasses which did not hide the bruise yellowing about her eye. Poor Janet!

Lucy sighed, took a mouthful of coffee and made a face. Neglected it had gone cold. A real friend went in even when she was unwelcome. After all it was herself she had not wished to embarrass. She would visit Janet.

Like themselves, Janet and Ewen were incomers, but that would not in itself have drawn them to the younger couple since the village was just near enough to act in part as a dormitory for the city.

'We have the rich,' Maitland would explain, 'a surgeon, a naval gent, a handful of company directors (one of whom is teetering on the verge of going broke our local bank manager tells me – in strictest confidence, naturally) – and they live behind walls or formidable hedges on the hill above the village. The poor cluster below it in council houses round the older of the two churches. There's something satisfying about having your class structure tidily analogous to the geography.'

More recently on the fields to the east there had been a development of large bungalows on small feus for supermarket managers and young accountants, a vet's widow, people like that. Like the Ures, Janet and Ewen Hayes were fortunate enough to live in the real village, on the straggling street which was the only one with any history to it. In the tiny pub beside the old manse house, Maitland would enjoy his occasional pint with farm labourers, a retired shepherd who had given up a job as a teacher after the war, Gordon who had sold the family printing business in Glasgow after his father's death and was drinking his way through the proceeds, Peter who owned the garage: a real cross-section. When Hugh talked about modernising the place to attract passing trade, Maitland would tell him he did not know the value of what he already had.

Glancing in through the gap in the curtained window she had a glimpse of the half-dozen regulars already crowding the taproom. All of them men, of course; it was that kind of pub. Perhaps that was what Maitland meant when he called it valuable. She smiled to herself and was surprised to find the doctor's wife smiling back as she hurried past.

In the dry morning light the village was sharp-cornered,

53

cold and clean. There was no wind and it looked as if the rain clouds might stay where they were, resting on the mountain summits across the strath. She went on the sunny side past the post office and the old tearoom now a Pakistani grocer's, and by the time she came to the terrace of cottages, three of which had been knocked together by Ewen Hayes, she was feeling better. The walk had done her good.

As she entered, she called out, but came at once on Janet curled up on the couch in the lounge with her head bent over a book. The red of her hair was vivid against a blanched prospect of winter garden.

'Enjoying a good book?'

'Oh, Jesus!' Janet cried out in fright.

'My dear!' Lucy said flustered. 'How stupid of me.'

But Janet, uncurling her long legs, was getting up, recovered and smiling. 'It's me who should apologise. You got more of a fright than I did. It's lovely to see you.'

'Country manners,' Lucy said ruefully. 'I did call out. But you were lost to the world. It must be good.' Curious she took up the book. It was a paperback with a cover showing a busty beauty in a Regency dress, hair wind-blown across a background of ships and swung cutlasses. It was not what she had expected to see and she began to read at the place where it had been laid open: 'Though she struggled against his grip and pled piteously, he drew her towards him inexorably. Slowly she was pulled down upon him and despite all her twisting the hard blade of his passion urged through the gossamer stuff of her gown against her straining thighs.' She felt her cheeks flush. Her eyes swept down the page: 'As he surrounded the soft peak of her breast with the hungry lapping of his tongue, a shudder passed through her and her thighs fell open. The throbbing heat of him thrust into her. A fierce reply rose to meet his driving need. The licking flames of desire – '

'Ohh!' she exclaimed, an unintentionally fastidious

sound, and dropped the book on the couch. 'I don't think I could cope with that so early in the day.'

'I believe they're known in the trade as bodice-rippers,' Janet said. 'Soft porn for stupid women.'

'But you're not a stupid woman.'

'No . . . I'm having another drink. Do you want to join me? Or is it too early for that as well?'

There was a glass on the coffee table beside the couch. She wondered how often it had been emptied already.

'Enough! – and lots of lemonade.' She settled into the chair opposite Janet on the couch. 'Cheers! I didn't feel like housework this morning.' Something ironical in the younger woman's gaze made her uncomfortable. 'It's been ages. Wherever does the time go?'

'Do you know what age I am?' Janet took a long swig from the glass as she waited for an answer.

'Not exactly.'

'I'm twenty-nine. I'll be thirty on the day before Christmas. That's my present for this year.'

Lucy was relieved. If that was all that was wrong!

'It's a present I'd be grateful for,' she laughed. 'It's rather too long since I woke up and found thirty in my stocking.'

'I don't want to grow old.'

'Oh, *old*!' Lucy cried, half amused and entirely offended.

Janet stared, absorbed and unsmiling.

'I go to sleep at night and wake up in the morning thinking about it. All those creams and the ghastly diets, you know? And exercise . . . Like men say, you know? are you fit? And that's what we pretend now too – that we're getting fit. Nobody ever says fit for what.' Involuntarily, Lucy glanced at the book on the couch; the bust spilling out of the Regency top defied nature. She could not bring herself to make the joke, but it would have been a relief if Janet had. Her tone was horribly serious. 'But it doesn't stop – you go on getting older every minute of every day – even while you're sleeping it doesn't stop . . . You leave an apple in the bowl and put fresh ones on top by mistake, and when you get to it it's gone black. Sometimes it looks all right – but the side you can't see is rotten. That's what's happening to us. We're rotting away.'

Alarmed, Lucy wished she hadn't come.

'I'm so frightened,' Janet said.

'But Ewen doesn't see you that way. He sees you as you are. He sees you as we all see you. He sees a beautiful woman.'

It wasn't her style to pay extravagant compliments and she believed this description to be true, though normally she would never have dreamed of saying so.

'How can you have any idea, married to Maitland, what a man like Ewen sees? I don't know how Ewen sees me any more. I know how he used to. When the business started, I did the books, I answered the phone. We'd sit at night and talk the day over – there wasn't anything came up we couldn't solve – it was hard going, but there was never any doubt we were going to make it. Then he didn't mind me playing up to men. Those fat old swine who hand out the contracts.' She smiled bitterly. 'I didn't go to bed with any of them. Not that I wasn't asked. That's one way for a young ambitious businessman to get his start, did you know that? I could point them out to you – you'd be surprised at the names. Big men now – but they pimped their wives to get there. To be fair the wives they have now aren't always the ones they pimped. But I just smiled and was nice. A pretty girl – it made them feel how important they were. Anyway they weren't all fat – quite dishy sometimes. Being rich suits the outdoor type. Ewen got his contracts – so many it didn't matter whether I was there or not. He's quite successful, you know.'

Lucy hesitated between admiration and commiseration, not sure which was being called for.

'He doesn't talk to me about the business now, or about anything much. He's got bigger – I've got smaller. There's nothing smaller than a housewife without children.'

'I don't feel that.'

'What?'

'I'm a housewife – it doesn't bother me. And I've got used to the idea we're not going to have a family. I don't feel worthless.'

'Oh,' vaguely, '. . . but you're different.' Before Lucy could decide on her reaction to that, she continued, 'You were at the Sinclairs'?'

'The Sinclairs'?' Lucy began, and then realising the potential for embarrassment if she took that line, went on firmly, 'Yes, we were there.'

'When I was dancing with Frank – it didn't mean anything. Christ, he's not even my type.'

'Oh, type.' I've never known quite what that meant, Lucy thought.

'I was lonely.'

Ewen had been there; not dancing with his wife or anyone else; settled morose in a corner brooding over his drink with a concentration that discouraged interruption. And then gradually everyone in the room was conscious of Janet as she danced with Frank Pritchard, everyone except her husband. Her body swaying, giving off the need and desire of a woman neglected; unselfconscious, lost and dreamily absorbed, she danced and Lucy had seen the faces of the men sweat and change and the women too watching her with a kind of greed. Then there was an inarticulate grunting and Ewen had pulled her from the floor. Everything went quiet, and as he realised what he had done his colour changed from red to a muddy white. But she had left, parting the silence, and at the door turned and drawled, Good-night all, *marvellous* evening. It had been a week before she ventured again on to the village street and the dark glasses only drew attention to the bruise around her eye.

'It's not as if he was interested himself,' Janet said. 'That little swine Scrope said to me, You did the women a good turn. Every wife in the village got screwed that night.' Lucy glanced away from her look of enquiry. 'Except yours truly.'

While she had been indoors, the clouds had crept across,

chilling the air. She pitied Janet. The grey light drained
everything of colour. She wondered if Ewen was as
successful as Janet believed. She had read somewhere that
more marriages break up over money than sex. That
seemed likely; but then it occurred to her that Janet might
have done more than smile and flatter those old men with
the power to put contracts Ewen's way.

Had she let them touch her? Those old gross men.

There was no way it seemed of controlling your
thoughts.

'Would you fetch my briefcase?' Maitland asked.

It was the comfortable time of the evening to which she
looked forward. They had brought through the percolator
and the little Dutch cups – windmills 4 and 6 of the set:
'Gronzeilermolen' and 'Stellingmolen' – to finish their
meal in front of the living-room fire. She had been
wondering if it would be disloyal to tell Maitland about
Janet, but wondering with the comfortable certainty that
she would, since she told him everything.

'You want me to get it?' The request puzzled her. 'But
where is it?'

'You didn't notice? I thought you might have. I put it
down when I came into the hall.'

'And you want me to get it?'

'Please.'

It crossed her mind she was being obtuse and spoiling
some surprise he had for her. The briefcase was lying on
the hall table. He had a new one, but still preferred this
battered old favourite in which he carried books and
papers, notes for talks and documents for Department
meetings. There was nothing lying beside it: she had
thought of chocolates; Maitland was fond of chocolates.
She hefted the weight of the case.

'I've poured coffee,' Maitland said.

'Lovely.'

He took the case from her without acknowledgement,

setting it on his knee and resting the delicate china cup upon it. She sipped her coffee, but the comfortable evening mood was spoiled. She waited.

'I had a seminar this afternoon,' Maitland said. He scraped the edge of the case with a fingernail. The sound affected her nerves unpleasantly. 'A group of bright young men – and women. Bright young people. I was reflecting on the Brothers Grimm. Would you believe, by the way, that not one of them could name one of Grimms' folk-tales, never mind having read them? "Cinderella . . .?" was one offering. Thank God, we didn't sink to Donald Duck.' And in his eager American voice, ' "Was that the guy who drew Snoopy, sir?" No, we're dealing with the cream of their generation. It's just that their generation hasn't been told about how the fearless boy learned fear or about the little girl who kept sticking her arm up out of the grave until they sent for her mother who came and whacked it down with a stick. Deprived. What do you think they had instead? The castles of Auschwitz and Dachau? Heinrich Himmler as hobgoblin? The German children of Grimm.'

'Wouldn't that be our generation?'

'Ancient history, you mean. And what will their children have? A video of *The Killing Fields* as a grotesquerie for the nursery?'

'Poor things – after all, they weren't expecting a seminar on folk-tales!' She laughed and felt better. Unlike Janet and Ewen Hayes their lives were not separate.

'In a way that was the point. They knew all about Grimm's law – voiceless stops and voiceless fricatives and the rest of it. Folklore and philology under the same hat – that's what I wanted them to think about. Those founding fathers were amateurs in a way it's not possible for any of us to be now. You get that lovely sense of the uncluttered power of the mind, pure logical intellect, that only comes from laymen busy inventing their science. Hutton in geology, Hugh Miller among his Old Red Sandstone; the assault of non-specialist reason upon the mysteries of nature.'

This tone of the lecture-room – he had too much of a sense of humour, too much of a sense of proportion for this. Uncertainly, she returned his smile.

'You might call it innocence. Who's been a bigger critic of the military-industrial complex than Noam Chomsky? And yet,' he reached a book down from the shelf, 'the research for *Aspects of the Theory of Syntax* was paid for by, let's see, "the Joint Services Electronics Programs (US Army, US Navy, and US Air Force) under Contract No. DA36–039–AMC–03200(E)". Money for science – yes, even linguistics, I say to them – came from the military, big money, in hopes of getting stuff that would be useful against "the enemy". And Chomsky hadn't been politicised yet by Vietnam. No discredit to him. But innocence gets harder to come by all the time. And after they'd talked themselves out, I decided to finish off by reading a couple of items. You know I do that – put things in the case to use in a seminar?'

Of course, she knew his habits. Alerted, she stared at the briefcase which he had set upright on his knee.

'I hadn't opened it till then. The Faculty meeting with McBain was postponed. Again!'

'Mmm.'

'So to make an end of the seminar, I tipped up the briefcase to bring out the papers. You know that trick of mine?'

He drew the low table up against his knees and, suiting the action to the word, emptied the case. A book and a selection of papers slid out, and with them slithering across the polished surface perhaps a dozen contraceptive sheaths in their neat little packages.

'That's exactly the way it happened.' He lined them up in a tidy row. *Now extra safe*, she read; *now extra safe*. 'I couldn't think of anything to say – and I'd been talking so fluently. My bright young people, being bright, took their leave. Being young they couldn't resist letting me hear their laughter from the other side of the door.'

60

'But it's disgraceful,' she said. 'How could they have dared?'

Nothing in her vision of Maitland with his students fitted a joke like that. If, in fact, it could be described as a joke at all. It was malice, the kind of malice directed against someone who was disliked and, worse than that, despised.

'But it's not funny, it's appalling,' she said.

'You don't feel I was over-reacting? I mean, to a student prank. Not in very admirable taste, of course, but then you don't look to students for models of taste.'

She was disappointed in him. It wasn't like him to look for some palatable evasion. 'I don't see how you can call it a prank!' she said.

'I'm not disagreeing,' he said mildly. 'I just wonder why you're so sure.'

'Those things,' her glance flicked over the neat row, 'those ridiculous things. They will make me embarrassed when we're on campus together. The idea someone might be referring to them when they see us.'

'You think they make me ridiculous?'

'That's not – not what I was saying—'

'They're dirty perhaps? But not ridiculous – in their right place. A place for everything and everything in its place.'

'I understand you must have been upset,' she said, 'but why take it out on me?'

'I couldn't think of anyone else who would have had the chance to put them in there.'

'You really are serious.' She knew that she should be more angry: the innocent should be angry. 'You really believe I could do a thing like that. Something so . . . undignified.' Suddenly she was in tears. 'If you don't—' And again, 'If you—' for what she could not find words for in her distress was this horror of not being known.

*

61

In the dark, his hand stroked her shoulder.

'You're not asleep?'

'No.'

He turned her gently and she felt his hand take the weight of her breast and then run lightly, tingling her skin, down her front until he trailed the tips of his fingers across her belly.

'You hurt me so much,' she whispered, and felt him stir against her.

'I'm sorry.'

'I don't understand how you could think a thing like that.'

'We'll call it a mystery. Let's not worry about it now.' 20All the time his fingers brought her to life. They stroked the inner side of her thighs, went on her belly, on her thighs again, on her groin. She opened to him. His finger lifted the sensitive beak of her flesh, rubbed.

'Come into me!'

'Roll over.' Still with his finger insistent on the sensitive place, he put her over face-down. She quivered knowing what was to come, and her buttocks sprang to the beating of his hand.

'I'm punishing you for what you did,' he whispered, his breath hot against her skin.

But, 'No!' she cried, and heaved herself away from him. How dare he! 'You said you believed me!'

'I'm sorry. I'm sorry.' His contrition whispered over her out of the dark. 'Sorry. Sorry. It's only our game. I wasn't talking about *that* – what happened. That's forgotten.' He kissed her on the lips. 'My darling, my love.' How could she help forgiving him? 'My love.'

His hands moved on her, but she could not see his face.

Later she woke and heard the deep rasp of his breathing and felt the weight of his leg across hers. At the moment of entering her, he had whispered something she hadn't made out and she'd thought, I can hardly ask him to say

62

it again, it's not the moment, and he had gone in, she had been afraid he wouldn't holding him to guide him in it had seemed too big in all the years it had never seemed so large, and he was in and she thought of how he would pull back to prepare the noise of the little packet tearing and the soft grunt and fumble of him as he drew it over himself but never so large as tonight would a sheath hold it? would it have burst in her? he was always so careful pressing out the air with his fingers so careful it would have been funny if funny if funny funny funny ah and the thick brute came as a stranger into the dance, forcing her, parting her, driving, driving, driving in. Until she milked the strength from it at last.

He had collapsed with his face nestled into her and perhaps he had slept for a moment for she had felt the water from his mouth dribble on to her shoulder and then he rolled away. And startled her with a noise she did not recognise at first as laughter. 'Remember the last night we made love? I'll bet every woman at the party got it that night – except poor Janet. There's no justice.' And laughed and yawned together.

She eased from under him gradually, intent upon not waking him.

In the bathroom the small mirror above the sink was not enough. She came out and into the guest bedroom where Monty Norman had slept. She drew the curtains before putting on the light. On the inner side of the wardrobe door there was a full-length mirror. She set it open and stood naked before it. On her left breast there was bruising round the nipple. She turned her breast to the light with trembling fingers. She twisted to glimpse the length of her back and buttocks. There was no mark on the white full flesh. She faced the mirror again and parting her legs saw the dark welts on her inner thighs.

She hated the pink-tinted, complacent image of her face in the glass. What did it have to do with her horror, with her fear? She had seen these bruises last night and they had not been caused by Maitland; they had not made love for weeks and in any case he was a gentle lover who would not do that to her. She had blamed him for accusing her — yet how could anyone tell what was behind that blankness caught in a mirror, frowning now as she had seen it frown over a menu for dinner? People slept defenceless by one another — ate what the other prepared — teetered side by side on cliff edges. Her body had been marked in some dream. If trust stopped, there was no safety anywhere. Oh, she should warn him there was malice in the world, warn him to be afraid.

Gently she touched the bruised nipple, comforting herself. She raised her head and saw Maitland's reflection. Her first instinct was to turn and hold out her arms to him, but she was ashamed of her nakedness. She had not taken her hand from where it cupped her injured breast, and now saw her free hand with an agonisingly slow furtive movement creep across and cover her sex.

The face of her husband watching seemed to her without expression, but then neither his own nor hers were flesh but only surfaces set side by side in a glass.

BOOK TWO

Something to Tell You

8

She wanted to cross the road. The car, though, had stopped in front of her and now as the woman got out a traffic warden had appeared.

'—not here, dear. You not see the double yellow line?'

As Lucy moved to go past, the woman swung the car door further open, blocking her way.

'Stopping on those lines could cause an accident,' the warden said. 'They're there for a purpose, you know.'

'Would you be quiet?' the woman said to him, and to Lucy, 'Don't go!'

'Are you drunk?' He pushed his face into hers and sniffed like a dog on a scent. 'If you're not safe, you shouldn't be in the vehicle.'

'I have to talk to you,' she said to Lucy.

'I'm talking to *you*. Are you listening to me?'

'Not really,' she said to him and pushed the door of the car shut. 'I'm going now and that'll let you get on with whatever you do.'

His voice followed them, 'I'll show you what I do,' but it sounded plaintive and deflated.

She had wanted to cross the road.

Why?

She was trying to think about this, and the woman was an interruption walking close to her, too close.

'There's somewhere I have to go,' Lucy said. 'I'm sorry I have no time.'

'Are you all right?' the woman asked. And Lucy recognised her. 'Are you all right?' Sophie Lindgren asked.

'I couldn't,' she felt sick, 'make up my mind where I wanted to go. Stupid – I was dreaming.'

'Were you going to visit the Trust?'

The girl was new, of course, and couldn't know how unlikely that would be.

'It's not a nice day,' Lucy said, looking around her. 'Not a day for shopping.' She felt her hair and the wetness of her cheeks. 'I've been walking in the rain.'

'You weren't coming to see me, were you?'

'What reason – Anyway how could I expect to see you here?' Lucy looked around. It was a street she did not recognise.

'Because I live near here. But, of course, you know that,' the girl was saying.

Something about where she lived? Was she trying to suggest she knew where she lived?

'But you do! I'm sorry. I mean, you were there with the Professor.'

Lucy shook her head. 'With my husband?'

Sophie Lindgren indicated, pointing along the street. 'There – just where the terrace goes up a level. That's the place. You can see the windows from here.'

And Lucy remembered. The kitchen with the dripping tap; the cheap reproduction pinned to a wall; the stale smell of cigarettes. She had gone there with Maitland and they had met – they had met—

'I could offer you a coffee,' Sophie Lindgren said. 'It's just across the road.'

There was somewhere she needed to go, was supposed to go. She couldn't think because of the girl. Question after question.

'A drink then? That might be better. You wouldn't want to get a chill.'

'I don't think so.'

'But you must! You've shivering. You'll make yourself ill.'

It seemed there was to be no peace. 'My husband suggested we buy one of the flats. As an investment. But he's not really a businessman.' She heard herself laughing and said, 'I think I should be going home.'

There was a place opposite, however, one of those squalid little hotels, and the girl was insisting.

'After all my dreaming,' Lucy said, 'it seems I've decided to cross the road.'

As she went up the hotel steps, noise jerked her head round. On a whooping double note the police car sliding from a side-street posted its ominous clamour ahead. Arms folded the warden stood across the street watching them.

The drink was very sweet. She didn't know what it was, and wondered if Sophie Lindgren had brought it without asking what she wanted. While she was thinking about that, the girl began to make sharp gasping sounds.

'I'm trying to picture May Stewart's face,' she said, and her shoulders shook with the little noises that although strange were more like laughter than anything else.

'Mrs Stewart?' The secretary at the Gregory and Rintoul Trust; it took Lucy a moment to place the name.

'It's her car, you see,' the girl said. 'Her lovely little Fiat with the what is it she calls it? two-colour toning. It'll be its very first parking ticket, I should think so, wouldn't you? with her being so careful, you wouldn't believe how careful she is.'

Perhaps she is drunk after all, Lucy thought. They had the lounge to themselves. Not even a man behind the bar; perhaps you rang a bell or something to fetch him out from wherever the music was clattering beyond the arch. 'You had Mrs Stewart's car?' It seemed so odd sitting alone with Sophie Lindgren. She really didn't want to be here.

'I've been dashing all over the place these last few days making final arrangements about taking the patients to the theatre. I even went to Balinter, to the University. I saw Professor Ure.'

'Oh, yes?' Lucy said vaguely. The table was scarred with small burns where cigarettes had been laid and the ash-trays were full – surely not from the previous night? and

69

then since the girl seemed to be waiting for her to say something else went on, 'And are you free today?'

'Oh, God, yes,' the girl said. 'I'm not cheating my employer. I'm not pretending to be ill. I'm free, if that's what you want to call it. I suppose you feel you have the right to ask that – I mean with being the Rintoul in Gregory and Rintoul.'

Twisting her mouth sourly like that quite spoiled the girl's prettiness and, startled, Lucy almost told her so but held back not wanting to be unkind. Instead, edging the stale ashtray away, she murmured half to herself, 'How surprised my husband would be to see me here.'

'He's been here,' the girl said. 'Sitting in that chair you're in now. But that was weeks ago, of course.' And tossed her head as if putting back a fall of long hair from her face, the same gesture as that first meeting at Waverley Station, waiting for her brother only there was no brother, it was Maitland who came off the train and – 'Did I tell you I've been arranging things?' she asked, leaning across the table. 'The theatre visit, things like that. I had to go and see Mr Chambers the lawyer. He's very protective of you.'

'I'm afraid I don't understand,' Lucy said.

'Oh, he made a point of it. He's known you all your life. Something about christening robes.'

'How strange . . .' That he should unburden himself to her. An old man with a pretty girl. She had thought better of him. 'He was always a remote figure to me. And yet perhaps . . . someone you've known when you were young is always – you imagine somehow, even so much later, that they're going to protect you or certainly like you . . . Isn't that so?'

'I wouldn't know,' Sophie Lindgren said. 'Maybe I knew different kinds of people when I was a child.'

'. . . You might be better prepared then.'

'Prepared?'

'For the things that happen . . . So perhaps I'm not so fortunate as you think.'

'Should I be sorry for you?'

The girl's impertinence made Lucy blink. 'Certainly not,' she said. 'In most people's terms I *am* fortunate. I have everything I want.'

'Don't other people have a right to be happy too?' Sophie Lindgren asked.

Self-evidently; and yet the girl was staring at her, fiercely, disconcertingly, waiting apparently for her to answer – as if it could possibly matter.

'I'm afraid,' Lucy said, 'I'm really not feeling particularly well.'

'It's just through the door – where we came in,' the girl told her.

The basin in the lavatory had no plug, but was choked with a couple of inches of grey scummy liquid. She dribbled water on to her fingertips and rubbed them across her forehead and temples. The floor of the cubicle was wet, the air smelled, but she sat in the cramped little box for a long time, until it became impossible.

It was no use. When she came out, Sophie Lindgren was there.

'I was out on the street looking for you,' she said. 'I thought you'd gone.'

'I should be going home.'

'It's still early.'

'I'm very tired.'

Too tired to resist.

Sophie Lindgren crossed to her and set the glasses on the table. She sat down and raised her glass.

'To happiness!' she said.

Lucy sipped at her drink. It was sweet and cloying and sickly on the tongue, like medicine in the nursery when no matter how sugary its deception you knew they had wrapped a bitterness inside.

'I have to tell you. Tell you everything,' Sophie Lindgren said. 'Believe me I don't want to hurt you.'

'Open your mouth, shut your eyes,' Lucy said. 'Like medicine.'

71

'Even if I have to force you, you're going to listen. It's wrong that you shouldn't know the truth.'

About what?

'What possible truth could you know that would matter to me?'

At the sour triumph of the other's smile, Lucy's breath stopped for fear.

Yet when the girl started to speak, it was about nothing – she had spent an evening with Monty Norman – weeks ago . . .

What was there to be afraid of in that?

BOOK THREE

Sophie Lindgren's Story

9

'It's my impression the Professor's the one who decides. Was he the one who gave you the job, Sophie? Was that the way it was?'

Though it was 'Sophie' and 'Monty' they were strangers still. As for the first names, he had insisted on them from the day a fortnight ago when he had started: 'Let's not have any of that Mr Norman stuff.' She smiled to herself. May Stewart's use of his first name was scarce; unspontaneous, you might call it. No doubt she felt threatened by him, even if it was still far from clear what he was actually there to do.

'Have you made up your mind?' Norman set down a pint glass and the whisky tumbler he had held pinned by his little finger. 'I've been feeding from the bowls on the counter.' In front of her he laid from his other fist a Martini and a packet of potato sticks. 'Funny place. Like drinking in a loo.'

The walls were tiled from floor to ceiling. Although the predominant impression was of dark green, the decoration of individual tiles was ornate Victorian: flowers, ships, stars.

'I love it.'

'Do a lot of your drinking in loos?' he asked.

'It's like being in a theatre.'

'A theatre loo.'

'No, seriously, it makes me think of a stage set. I can't think what kind of play though.'

Instead of pursuing the notion, he reached over and tore open the sticks packet. 'Have one.'

'I'm not hungry.'

'Keep you from getting hungry. End of the working day.'

She drew out one of the sticks. Apart from their own the tables were unoccupied. At the shorter of the bar's counters, round the corner out of view came the muttering of men's voices. The barman leaned with his hands on the counter, head bowed as if praying for custom.

'Back to the question,' he said. 'What brought you to work there? Bright ambitious girl like you. It's only a clerking job, isn't it?'

'Actually, I replaced two part-timers. So there's plenty to do.'

'But you've "actually" got a degree, haven't you?'

'For what it's worth.'

'From – what do you call it?'

'Balinter.'

'There you are then. Same place as the Professor's at. You could do better than clerking.'

'It's only an ordinary degree. People who graduated same time as me don't have a job at all yet.'

'What time would that be?' Then before she could answer, he said abruptly, 'You're spoiling it.'

She did not understand till he pointed at the potato stick she was turning in her fingers. She dropped it in the ashtray. 'I'm not hungry.'

'Nobody'll get it now,' he said with a frown. 'You were saying when you graduated?'

'Just in June.' It seemed to her that made it more plausible that she should be working for the Trust. 'I started in September.'

'So you'd done a bit of looking first – over the summer?'

She hesitated. 'I gave myself a holiday first.'

'So you weren't too worried.' He drew out a bundle of the potato sticks and held them out to her. She shook her head in refusal. 'About getting a job, I mean.' He tilted his head and the sticks slid between his lips.

'I'd promised myself a holiday.'

'You knew something would turn up.'

'I suppose so.'

'Did the Professor say there'd be a job for you?'

'There was an advertisement – I applied.'

Taking more of the sticks, he turned the bag towards her. She shook her head.

'Still, with being at the same university, knowing him, it can't have done your chances any harm.'

'I was in one of his classes. It would be a bit grand to say I knew him.'

'You and me both.' Monty Norman looked at her in triumph.

'Sorry?'

'Both of us got our jobs through the Professor. It gives us something in common. Makes us allies.' He smiled. 'You should share these with me, one bite. Make us blood brothers – like the Red Indians.'

Irritated, this time she pushed the packet back across the table to him. He looked at it, chewing his lip. 'What do you make of the Stewart woman then?'

'May,' she reminded him with a touch of malice.

'Her. She's not easy to be jolly with.'

The phrase made her laugh. 'She's all right. She regards the Trust as Good Works. That's why she does it – I'm sure she could get more money somewhere else.' Realising that might be tactless, she hurried on. 'She may not be very lively, but she does her job well.'

'You think so?'

She looked at him in surprise. 'Don't you?'

He poured potato sticks into his palm. 'Sure you don't want a taste of one of these?'

'Positive.'

'You have a lot of will-power,' he said thoughtfully.

'Because I won't have a potato stick?'

'Right.' He chewed with a crunching sound. A fleck of dry crumbs showed at one corner of his mouth.

'They're just not the kind of thing I enjoy.'

'You're stubborn,' he said. 'It doesn't embarrass you to be stubborn.'

'If you think it's important.' On impulse, she picked one of the sticks from his palm and ate it. 'I'm not on a diet or anything.'

'Now I'm not sure who's won,' he complained.

For a moment she imagined he was serious and then decided to appreciate his sense of humour and laugh.

'Of course, as far as judging May's work,' he reflected, 'like you say, you haven't been there long yourself.'

'She's efficient. It doesn't take long to tell that.'

'You like her.'

'Well, I don't not like her.'

'And the Professor?'

'I don't know whether he's efficient. Ask May!'

'No. I meant, do you like him?'

'Do we have to talk shop? We're not in the office now.'

'. . . Fine. Something else to drink?'

'I'll get them.'

But he took the money from her hand. 'You sit and relax. I'll bring them.'

'Fine,' she said, borrowing the word from him. Accepting his invitation for a drink had seemed simpler than refusing. But quite apart from the legitimate reasons for disliking him – above all that Maitland had complicated things so horribly by sticking him into a room in the flat – he got on her nerves unreasonably.

A surreptitious check on her change suggested he had paid for almost all of that round also.

'I wanted a double,' he said, as if reading her mind. 'I let myself be old-fashioned and paid for it.' He closed his fists and, grinning at her, mimed a boxer defending himself. 'We can call it a draw.'

As she was puzzling over what on earth he was talking about, she heard the unmistakable voice of Viv Law. In the last few minutes the bar had begun to fill, and most of this change she now saw had been caused by the arrival of a group of about a dozen people. In the centre of them a thin woman in her early fifties was patting with yellow fingers at wisps of hair drawn out in untidy strands.

'That's Viv Law just come in,' she said. 'At the table behind you.'

'Who?'

'Viv Law. She's a journalist. She does work on occasion to help out at the Trust. The good cause thing again. I doubt if she gets paid. Of course, she's a friend of Professor Ure's.'

'For someone who hasn't been there long, you have it all taped,' he said admiringly.

You'd be surprised how much I know, she thought. About Viv Law, for example. I know why she left the magazine she helped to start; I know how much she loved her father and why she was at odds with her mother; I know why she turned down that advertising job in London. I know – a number of things, but not how to explain that I know any of them.

But while she was puzzling over that, Sophie found a sharp narrow-eyed gaze fixing her and then the older woman was on her feet and approaching.

'Aren't you with the Gregory and Rintoul?'

The question was abrupt, with an edge to it that sounded unfriendly.

Something else I know, Sophie remembered. Viv Law has a hell of a temper.

'I've seen you there – May Stewart introduced us. I don't remember your name.'

'I thought journalists never forgot a name,' Monty Norman said with a smile.

'You're thinking of fucking politicians,' Viv Law said, and turning back to Sophie went on, 'I've just come from the Trust office. I had something to hand in.'

'I could take it,' Sophie said helpfully. 'I'll give it to May in the morning. If that would help?'

'Oh, I saw May. I'd phoned her I was bringing it in.

Only it turns out there's a little problem. It's not needed. Who is this shit Norman who's fucking the place up?'

Her voice went up another notch and the group stopped even pretending not to listen. It was clear they knew Viv gave good value.

'I'm that shit Norman.'

'Yes. I thought you might be.'

'What's your problem?'

'I'm a busy woman,' Viv Law said with an unpleasantly reasonable air. 'I don't like to have my time wasted.'

'You don't have to be a woman to feel that,' Norman said.

'I knew I wasn't going to like you.'

'If there's been some kind of mistake,' Sophie tried to intervene, not for Norman's sake but for the Trust's or rather for Maitland's since it was what he might have wished her to do.

'Not by me, love. I was *asked* to do that circular. You know, to the welfare clubs? For the Christmas appeal.'

'Well?' Norman asked, but both women had caught his involuntary flicker of response. If he didn't know before, Sophie thought, he does now what this is about. She, however, was still in the dark.

'I took them to the post yesterday,' she soothed. 'They've gone off in good time.'

'Too fucking good. That's what I was taking in today – the day I was asked to bring it in – the copy for it. I spent last night on it. It's only amateurs think you can do these things in five minutes. And that's what you've sent out, love – an amateur's piece of bloody silly-clever.'

'I wrote the letter,' Monty Norman said. 'That's part of my job. Nobody told me you'd been asked.'

'Don't give me that crap! May Stewart told you.'

Sophie was startled by a glance at her of pure malevolence from him. Did he blame her for witnessing this?

Next moment he was smiling. 'Let's not argue,' he said, 'whether she did or not. Mostly she does her job splendidly. I've no desire to cause trouble for her. I don't think

80

I made such a bad job of the letter – but I'd be glad of your help with the next one.'

'I'm a professional,' Viv Law said. 'Maitland Ure asked me to do something. A date came with it. All right, I get it done and I get it done on time. But the other side of that is that I don't get messed about.'

'I'll make you a suggestion. There's time enough before Christmas.' And in an aside to Sophie, 'You were a bit hasty, you know, getting them posted. We'll give it a fortnight and then we'll send your letter out as a follow-up. Ginger them up a bit. That way nothing's wasted.' He nodded up at her with a hint of complacency.

'Oh, you're something,' she said unexpectedly quietly.

Her rage as she descended on them had been histrionic and seemingly instantaneous. As suddenly as it had blown up, it had dissipated, leaving her yellow and unwell-looking.

'That's such a bad idea for so many reasons.' With a kind of resentful self-consciousness, she tucked back a wisp of straying hair. 'No way any letter of mine is going out after that bloody shambles of yours. The only consolation is that nobody could think it had anything to do with me. So let's not get anybody confused, just in case. Tell Maitland Ure I won't be writing anything else – not while you work for the Trust.' Turning away, she added abruptly, 'Never mind! I'll tell him myself.'

'Whatever you like.'

Monty Norman raised his glass in an ironical toast to the watching group, but that was a mistake. His eyes returned to Sophie too quickly for her to change the direction of her gaze. The amber liquid slopped to and fro in the glass but instead of putting it down he held it while the trembling slowed. When it stopped, he held out the glass with his arm at full stretch and nodded at the steadiness of his hand.

With his free hand he pushed the packet of potato sticks across to her.

'Have one,' he said. 'Before they're finished.'

81

10

'He was so angry, I think he could have killed her.'

'Viv flies off the handle but it doesn't last. I've seen her incandescent and a week later best friends with the victim. If you'd seen the rage, you'd have sworn it was deadly earnest. And permanent.' He yawned. 'I'll smooth her feathers. It isn't important.'

The tickle of his breath by her ear accompanied the low comfortable monotone. She had learned that the sweetest time for her came after they had made love. She had not been a virgin when they first went to bed a year ago, but at twenty she had had only two others with whom to compare him. As a first-year student she had been taken against a wall after a party. She had been drunk and giggling. 'Oh, is that your finger? That's only your finger still, isn't it?' Then she had felt the thick pressure of the boy nuzzling his way into her, and that clumsy entry intermingled always in her memory with the sour clogged flow of his breath into her face. In her inexperience, she had no idea of how far in he might be; but she was sobered out of any misapprehension about fingers. Panic-stricken, she shoved at him, twisting and writhing away as he grunted with pain. A tall boy with blond hair, he had told her he was Norwegian and at the party had spoken in broken English, encouraging her to say things recklessly in the belief he would not understand. Now out of his mouth in the broadest of Glasgow accents came the words: 'Ya cock teasan stupid cunt.' The first blow stunned her with shock so that the rest followed in a single confusion of pain and terror. Perhaps altogether there were no more than six, delivered with the open hand but each one as a fully swung blow. The slap which put her down took her high on the side of the head, and he caught her with another one as she fell. The whole thing took hardly any time at all; his reflexes were very good. Crouched against the bottom of the wall, she wept with relief as he walked away. In the morning she found blood caked at the side of her mouth, but no show of it on her underwear. Under the circumstances, it was difficult to decide if she had stopped being a virgin. After that she did see him about the campus, and it dismayed her that he gave no sign either of remorse or apprehension. On the other hand, he did not try to approach her and she was grateful for that. She was the one who suffered disgust and even guilt. She lost confidence. She had waking fantasies of giving in to him, of doing whatever he asked, of him leading her into a room of his friends, of her humiliation; but twice she wakened out of dreams in which she had killed him. He lay dead at her feet and she wakened suddenly with a feeling of glory that changed at once into terror. Because her retreat had been into work and hard study – since she was basically very sensible, with a sharp sense of the distinction between fantasy and reality, and an instinct for self-preservation – she did well at the sessional exams; and that helped more than anything. In her second year she developed a social life and, out of a circle of friends, a recognised boy friend emerged, a diffident redhead immersed in junior honours economics. Urged on by the habit of the time, they arrived in bed together and after several failures made love; and, pleased with themselves, did so on a number of occasions after that, even though by some accident of chemistry the experience for both of them was disappointingly humdrum. All the same, it seemed they were ready to drift out of affection into something they would have called love; but the habit of study had stayed with her from that unhappy first year and at the end of the second she won the class prize. It was this which had drawn her to Maitland's attention.

'Have you fallen asleep?' Gently he rocked her in the nook of his arm.

'Dreaming.' She turned her head and raising herself licked her tongue like a cat along the muscle of his chest. His flesh smelled sweet to her but his taste was salt. 'I dreamt I could eat you.'

For answer he caught her by the nape and shook her playfully. His grip was powerful and gentle at the same time; he was like a lion. It was a comparison she would have blushed to use aloud, even to him in this intimacy. Least of all to him: she could imagine his shout of laughter; imagine the slyly conscious profile he would offer to her of the romantic hero. She would not risk that he should learn the beginning of despising her. It pleased her in her thoughts that he should be a lion. By the tender kneading grip he had taken of her she let herself be pressed close until, mock menacingly, she worried the hard little button of his nipple between her teeth. After they had made love was the sweetest time for her.

'But it wasn't her, it was him who was so angry.' She laid her head on his chest. 'After she went back to her own table, I would have got up and left if I had been him, but he stayed and kept smiling and talking at me. The whole thing made me ravenous and I told him I had to go and eat. But he wouldn't leave – it was so childish. He wouldn't go.'

'Pride. She had to leave before he would.'

'As if that would prove anything. Anyway, they were settled in for the evening as far as I could see. Maybe they'd eaten before they came in or maybe they didn't need food as long as they could drink. My God! that crowd could drink. And the place kept getting more and more crowded. It was all smoke and voices and glasses banging down. I began a headache. And every time that gang behind laughed about something – I don't know how to describe it, his face went stiff. And then he'd smile and begin to talk very fast. It got to the stage I'd had enough. I couldn't take any more. I walked out and left him to it.'

Maitland was amused. 'Poor devil! I don't imagine he's run up against many like Viv in full song.'

'You didn't see his hand shaking.'

'A bad case of wounded vanity.'

'Rage. Apart from his hands he could hide it. But he couldn't stop his hands from shaking.'

'I wish you'd stayed. I'd dearly like to know what happened after you left.'

'He told me the next day.'

'. . . So?'

'He outstayed them – after they left, he left.'

His chest rose and fell, lifting her head on the little coughing spasms of laughter. 'The drama ends in anticlimax.'

She lifted herself so that she could watch his face. 'He tried to get into my room when he came back.' He let the last dribble of laughter go and sighed. 'It was late. He tried the door but I'd put the lock on.'

Maitland rolled away from her and got out of the bed. He had strong shoulders and the muscles on his back tightened as he stretched his arms and yawned. She wanted to touch the hard white rounds of his buttocks. She wanted him to come back to bed; she wanted to take his weight upon her again. Pulling on his shirt, he said, 'If he was trying the handle of your door after a night's drinking, I shouldn't imagine it was anger that was bothering him.'

'Is that what was supposed to happen?'

In the act of buttoning the shirt, his hands stilled. 'That's an interesting tone.'

She swallowed but went on, 'Was I supposed to let him make love to me?'

His hands moved again, quickly, fastening the buttons into place. 'It wouldn't have pleased me, no. My tastes are less esoteric.'

'I don't understand why you brought him here.'

'I seem to remember, my pet, it was you who told me

there was a room available. Because that girl – the one who cluttered up the loo with quack remedies for acne – had gone back to her parents.' She watched as with deft intent movements he knotted his tie before the mirror. She had a desolate sense of him armouring himself against her.

'Only for something to tell you.' A scrap of gossip from the meagre area where his life, so full and rich, overlapped with hers. Didn't he understand? 'I never expected – did you put him in here so you would have an excuse to stop seeing me?'

'I'm here,' he said. 'If I can trust my own sensations, I'm just out of your bed.'

'Because I *asked* you to come. When I was sure he wouldn't be here.'

'Having other people around hasn't bothered you before.'

'Who was I to worry about? Poor Jackie with her spots? Or Pat and the little bald man? Did you know she comes in here all the time to moan about him?' And she couldn't stop herself, heard her voice offering him another of her poor scraps of gossip. 'She said to me, "He thinks living together means when he says, I'm going to London for the weekend, I run and pack his case." Were we supposed to be worried by *them*? Or the Irish boy who's trying to be a painter?'

'Perhaps we should stop seeing one another, if this isn't fun for you any more.'

'Fun!' But now she was in tears. She drew the sheet up over her breasts as if to hide from him, armoured against her in his other existence. She had seen him with the same look, it struck her now, listening to a seminar paper, deciding while he waited for it to end what he would say to get what he wanted.

'I like risk,' he said. 'Norman being here adds to the fun – adds a little spice.'

'You make me feel dirty.'

'Very liberated.'

'I don't want to be liberated,' Sophie said. 'I don't want

86

you to get up after we make love and walk away from me. I don't want to be left in this terrible room. I don't want to be alone.'

—I want to be married. I want to be married to you.

She was at the centre of silence. Encompassing her and flowing out from them was the infinite sphere of his stillness, holding them within it, dwindled figurines of male and female, waiting upon change and the event.

There was no way she would ever give him up. Truth was not something you turned your back on once it had been found. His marriage had failed or why would he need her? She would bring him a new life. Her womb stirred. Whatever she did was for him.

If she had to fight for her happiness, she would fight.

11

Maitland had told her: when he slips down in his seat, right down, that's when I keep my eye on him in the Committee. When he does that, he's passing judgement. Once he's decided what it should be, he delivers it with an upward glance – not the judgement of a moralist *de haut en bas* – but of an appraiser, you see, an old jurist. Settled down like that, he's weighing actions against consequences. It's a chilly judgement and he passes it on himself as well as others.

But perhaps, after all, this judgement was not to be passed on her.

'Mr Norman had to be out of the office today. And it was only when I was ready to leave, practically out of the door, that May – Mrs Stewart – suggested . . .'

She trailed off, under his eye conscious of the muddle she was making of this.

'Mr Norman doesn't know you are here.'

She assented. It was what she had been trying to say.

'In this case, we may say it is *jus tertii* to him who you may visit before your expedition to the west.'

Expedition to the west? Of course, she had told him she was on her way to Glasgow. Christ!

'You understand the term?'

Expedition? She stared at him puzzled, and then the penny dropped.

'I gave Latin up at school.'

'But I thought your degree was in languages.'

'An ordinary degree.' Why the hell did she say that? It

wasn't the point. 'The classes I did – in linguistics – they were about the grammars of English. Jespersen. Halliday. Chomsky.'

' "Grammars".' Yes, in the plural. She watched him thinking about that; but he was too canny to pursue it. 'The phrase simply means – it doesn't concern him. It's no business of his whether you are here or not.'

Oddly enough, the exchange eased some of her tension. There had been a friend of her father's, a retired headmaster, who had addressed her in much the same way when she was a girl: Ist der Tee kalt? Don't tell me you have no German? Possibly Italian? A little Hebrew perhaps? Don't be upset by him, her mother had said. It's just his way of trying to talk to you. He's never found it easy to communicate with young people.

The resemblance, however superficial, however deceptive, comforted her.

'I assume Mr Norman would see it like that?' Julian Chambers asked.

'That it wasn't any of his business?' She saw that he was waiting for something further. 'Mostly I get told what to do by Mrs Stewart. Like today. To deliver the proofs for Mr Terence's thesis and the pamphlets for Mrs Gray in connection with the new hospice ward. Not that they couldn't be posted—' and stopped, realising that sounded like a criticism.

'Mr Norman has no duties for you?'

'He hasn't been there very long.'

'Three weeks and two days.' With a bony knuckled finger he stroked back one leaf of the desk diary.

'I did think there would be more for me to do with him there . . . He seemed to have a lot of ideas.'

'But in the event not so many after all.'

Was this why May Stewart had packed her off today; so that she could be questioned about Monty Norman? Sophie decided on caution. 'He's – it's not really very long.'

She was unpleasantly conscious of the old lawyer's high

pale brow. His thinning white hair drawn back fiercely from it accentuated its height. Because he sat so low in his seat, she could see the shine of his scalp, the skin of it by contrast gleaming pink and healthy. He must really be a very healthy old man with that pink gleaming scalp and the flexible spine of a boy that let him slump like that and gaze up so steadily at her. She wondered what age he was in fact. Seventy? But if someone had told her eighty she would have believed them.

'You know how much a scandal would damage the Trust?' he asked.

A flush like guilt went through her.

'Reputation is a fragile commodity,' he said. 'Made over years, lost in days.'

There was nothing she could offer to that.

'You came to the Trust through a recommendation from Maitland.'

'Professor Ure. Yes.'

'Maitland.'

His insistence on the name troubled her. Such informality must be uncharacteristic.

'Mrs Stewart seems satisfied with what I do,' Sophie said. 'I think we get on well together.'

Julian Chambers frowned. It is as if, she thought, anything I say is only an interruption.

'When the Trust began, there was a difficulty. The elder Rintoul – Lucy's grandfather that is – Lucy, Mrs Ure? . . . yes – he was a self-made man, and self-taught too, but his prosperity was founded on patents; he was a brilliant engineer. By contrast, Charles Gregory was a surgeon, and a very distinguished one. Different professions and so different objects in their philanthropy. Logically, separate trusts would have been the simplest answer. But they were friends. They wanted their names to be linked. As it was drawn up at first, their charitable purposes were stated disjunctively and the problems that error created might well have seen the Trust extinguished before it was properly started.'

90

He looked at her as if to say, You see? but, of course, she did not.

'A direction of that kind can become void for uncertainty since it would allow trustees to favour one object to the exclusion of the other – assuming that is they are truly alternative, and certainly Gregory's medical philanthropy and Rintoul's desire to encourage industrial innovation were. Hardly could be more obviously so.'

Not being a fool, she had begun to follow; but what she could not see was why he should be explaining all this for her benefit.

'That was corrected – the disjunction – and both objects became and have remained legitimate concerns of the Trust. The coming of the National Health Service, however, wasn't something Gregory had foreseen. The Trust invoked the *cy pres* principle and the Inner House of the Court of Session found for us. That let us go on, you see, in the spirit of what Gregory intended, to meet situations of which he had no cognisance. We took a very early interest in the hospice movement. As the years pass, I begin to think of it as the best part of our work.'

He paused and drew his lips together as if annoyed with himself over an indiscretion; and that made her realise: Being old is what he's thinking about. Being ill and old and needing help in learning how to die.

'By its very nature, Rintoul's desire to further innovation meant movement in the objects of benefaction.' He made a face, involuntarily it seemed, as if the idea of necessarily implied change was distasteful. 'Like Mr Terence's thesis there, computers for the blind, the talking terminal, what pleasure it would have given those two friends to find the really rather ill-matched objects of their philanthropy coming together in that way.'

There was a pause which went on until she ventured, 'It's very interesting,' and understood from the blankness of his stare that this was not the point.

'I am anxious,' he said, 'that you should feel what the Trust is, not something dead but a responsibility going on

91

through time. The benefits of a private trust accrue only to individuals, who die and the trust with them. The trust which benefits the public, however, need have no set time of ending. To go on indefinitely, that's a kind of immortality by *actio popularis*. You don't think that's too fanciful?'

The word applied to anything he might say amused her. She shook her head, smiling.

'To my mind, it resembles the condition of marriage. Marriage begins with a contract – its intentions, deriving from a preceding situation, are framed at that moment of ceremony – but time passes. There's the test. When changes come, the marriage has to cope. If it does, time, you may say, enriches it. The relationship simply goes beyond, bursts the boundaries, of those original intentions; but not of the contract, the ceremony, which has taken account of all that possibility of growing, to the end of time and beyond. Yes . . .' He lapsed into some private thought of his own, then, returning, shot her a sharp glance. 'I am speaking of the ceremony, the contract, of a Christian marriage.'

Of Maitland's marriage.

'Yes.' She managed the single dry syllable as he waited, the blank white wall of his forehead raised against her.

After all she was the one this old man had chosen to judge.

May Stewart that day in the office not introducing her to Maitland's wife, *she* had known. Yet the secretary had seemed to take to her from the first morning. They had got on so well together. Had she really been stupid enough to imagine she had made some kind of ally of May Stewart, devoted May, devoted to Maitland – Stupid! Contradictory images tumbled through her head, of Maitland loving her, of Maitland in her arms, of Maitland speaking of anything and everything under the sun except the life he led with his wife. That dull ageing woman! If Maitland was too loyal, she did not have to be told to know how he must feel. *Must*. Let her marry Maitland and she would show this lawyer with his contracts and ceremonies what love meant. Hadn't Maitland the right to be happy?

Opening her mouth to speak, she was forestalled. 'You mustn't let me bore you,' Julian Chambers said, 'about the Trust. I wanted you to understand the very particular feeling some of us have for it. There must not be any risk, however remote, of scandal. That's why Mr Norman won't be allowed to sign cheques.'

Expecting anything but this, she was disconcerted.

'You didn't know?' Chambers speculated. 'I had the impression from Mrs Stewart that you knew.'

'I might have heard something.' Her mind had stopped working. She struggled to find something sensible to say. 'The pair of them talking . . . I didn't feel it was any of my business.'

'Mrs Stewart has authority to draw upon the Trust account for routine payments below a certain level. That is a matter of administrative convenience. Above that sum, as normal practice, other signatories would be required for confirmation. In any case, whatever the sum there is no need for Mr Norman to be involved.'

As he finished abruptly, she was conscious only of her own relief. All her guilty imaginings had been nonsense. It was shameful that she should have let it happen, for she felt no guilt; there was no reason for her to feel guilt. None of this had anything to do with her, only with Monty Norman. Not judged, she was being treated as a confidante. Here was something she would share with Maitland. It would have been easy for her to weep.

As Julian Chambers rose to his feet, she stood also.

'I have no intention of impugning Mr Norman's honesty. The point is general. It would be rash to give it any particular application to Mr Norman. I wouldn't want to be misunderstood.'

She nodded without entirely following what he was saying. Beside his tallness, the emotion she felt was a deception of memory. Her father's friend, the headmaster, avuncularly towering had bent down to joke with her.

93

Kaffee für mich, bitte, es ist zu kalt für Bier und Wein. Don't tell me you have no German. A little Hebrew perhaps?

'Have you met Mrs Ure?'

'I'm sorry?'

'Maitland's wife.'

'She came to the office – and for the last meeting.'

'She is a very fine person. A lady – if you will allow me that expression from another time. I have known her for a great many years. All of her life, indeed. I am very fond of Lucy. You understand?'

From his great height, balefully, he had left no room for doubt.

Beyond any hope of a mistake, Sophie understood why she had been summoned.

12

When the door opened, it was May Stewart, who raising her hand to her lips cried, 'Did I startle you? I got a fright myself – I was sure you had gone out for lunch without saying.'

'No . . .' She looked at her watch: it was after one. 'Is it so late?'

'Are you feeling unwell again? You shouldn't have come in today.'

Mr Terence's thesis leaned forlornly against the bundle of undelivered hospice material on the table.

'We'll post them,' May Stewart had said in the morning; but now they had missed the first collection. 'And Mr Chambers? You didn't see him either?'

'It was after I saw him I felt sick and had to go home,' Sophie had told her vindictively.

'Did he speak to you . . . about Mr Norman?'

'There wasn't a lot I could tell him. Mr Norman has a lot of good ideas. I told him that.'

'Do you know he wants to sign the cheques?'

'Well, you do.'

'That's not the same! I've worked fifteen years for the Trust. It means something to me. Anyway, only up to a hundred pounds.'

'It's between you two, isn't it?'

'But I can't just let things go. I have a *responsibility*. And another thing – he comes in when he likes. I've always worked regular office hours, though I needn't have. No one was here to bother. I just wouldn't have felt it was right.'

Sophie had escaped then, and been left alone in the workroom to brood.

Now May Stewart was asking again, 'You're all right?'

'I didn't sleep well last night.'

To offer that was weak, an excuse; like the ones she had made all her life, to her parents, to schoolteachers, to lecturers at Balinter. The habit of apologising was a hard one to break, no matter how angry you were, how full of contempt.

'Have you eaten yet?'

'I'm not hungry.'

The secretary shepherded her along the corridor to her own room. 'Fruit and biscuits,' she said. 'I always bring too much. You can share and then we'll make coffee.'

Into two round plastic containers, she sliced apple, banana and a peach carefully divided between them. She handed one over.

Staring into the little bowl, Sophie explained, 'I'm not hungry. I think I'll go for a walk – don't worry, I won't take too long.'

A light flush touched the secretary's fine high-boned cheeks. 'I rather thought, Sophie, you and I had become friends.'

Sophie put a piece of the fruit into her mouth. The chunk of banana was slippery and tasteless.

'Last week,' she said, 'Monty Norman tried to get me to share a bag of potato sticks. Apparently that would have made us blood brothers.'

'Blood brothers?'

'Allies, I suppose he meant.'

'Why should he suppose you would want to be an ally of his?'

'Perhaps because we both owe our jobs to Professor Ure'; and added deliberately, 'Maitland.'

'It's so wrong, Sophie,' May Stewart said. 'You don't have to put it into words. I know how you must feel about the man.' Then as Sophie stared, she cried out, 'He's an *impossible* man!'

With the side of her fork, Sophie cut into the soft flesh of the peach. She did it automatically, working out that it was Monty Norman who was impossible, but the juice of the peach ran between her teeth and the rich sweetness of it surprised her into pleasure. She cut another piece and popped it into her mouth, and looked up to find the secretary smiling at her.

'Thing is, the first time I saw him he reminded me of the Professor. I was sure I was going to like him. Isn't that silly?'

'They couldn't be more unlike.'

'I haven't put it into words,' May Stewart said, 'but it's been so nice to have young company. I love this job, no two days are the same – well, you've found that out – but the one drawback was the lack of company, apart from the odd temp or a bit of part-time help. Not the same thing, is it? And then you came. I was so pleased.'

Why try to get rid of me then? Sophie wondered. Why tell Chambers about Maitland and me, you evil old bitch?

'You're not at an age when you'll ever lack company,' the secretary was going on. 'For me I suppose you could say the Trust fills a gap. I still miss my husband, though it's a long time since he died.'

If he died, Sophie reflected maliciously. If he didn't run away; if, that is, he ever existed at all. She wouldn't be the first old maid to invent a husband.

'I haven't heard you talk about him before.'

'He was the kindest of men. Of course, my friends didn't want me to marry him. They meant well. As if I didn't know everything they could whisper to me against it. He was already in a wheelchair – the illness had got to that stage. At the most, they told me I could only hope for two years with him. But we proved them wrong. He lived for almost five years after we were married. It was a kind of miracle, they said. Someone called it once the power of love, and that meant so much to me. People say things to us we never forget for good or ill. The power of love . . . I had been a nurse, of course.'

'I can't picture that.'

'Oh, yes. That's where we met – in hospital. After he – afterwards I couldn't bear to go back though. I don't know why. I'd had enough of it, I suppose.' She smiled. 'I've sometimes thought, you know, perhaps I was afraid if I went back into hospital work I would meet someone else – someone ill, of course – and fall in love again. Nurses are fools in that way.' In alarm, she shook her head. 'But don't misunderstand! I wouldn't have married anyone else. Not really ever, I don't think. Jerry spoiled me for anyone else. Such a kind man.' And then casually, softly, as if to herself, but fixing Sophie with a look that would not be denied, she went on, 'He was paralysed even when I met him, before I married him – from the waist down. There never was any question of – I don't know anything about that side of life. Despite the Mrs.'

In this office there were no windows to the outside. The untouched pieces of apple in the bowl had turned brown under the white lamp.

'Oh, Sophie,' the secretary said, 'don't waste your life. You know what love is, but you don't know what loneliness is. Don't let yourself be lonely.'

'I think I'll take that walk now,' Sophie said getting to her feet. The secretary's face tilted palely up to her. 'Maybe I'll buy a magazine, one of those woman's ones, the advice columns always make me laugh.'

Later, her head buzzing with words, she would think of funnier things, angrier things, more dignified things. But on the spur of the moment, it had to do and, from the look on May Stewart's face, it seemed to be enough.

In the conference room, she taped the bundles and addressed them, and kept one eye on the door. Everything took a long time; she kept getting things wrong and redoing them, determined there would be no faults to find. Wearied, she looked down into the service area. Rain was seeping on to the sodden remnants of cardboard boxes.

When the door opened, she swung round, startled into the habit of excusing herself, 'I've finished all I had to do.'

'Good for you,' Monty Norman said, not coming in. 'Is May in her office?'

'I can't think where else she would be.'

'I've done a good morning's work,' he said, standing in the doorway, rubbing his chin and watching her. 'I had some leads I wanted to follow up. You and May must have wondered where I was. You'll be surprised. Things are going well. You know like the song says? – "There's a good time just around the corner". I didn't hear you come in last night.'

The suddenness of the transition confused her. 'Come in?'

'To the flat. No two people walk the same way. Everybody's footsteps coming into the hall, I know them now. I said to myself, Sophie's making a night of it.'

'You didn't hear me because I was already there. I came home in the afternoon. I didn't feel well.'

He blinked. 'You were there all the time? Me listening and you were there all the time.'

The intentness of his gaze made her uneasy. He put his hand into his pocket and then held it up with the back towards her. When he turned it, she saw that he had a packet of contraceptives held by the squeeze of his palm like a conjuror. He held it between finger and thumb and seemed to take it with his other hand, but it was empty and then he showed her that both were.

'I expect I'll find something to do with them. The joke's on me,' he said. 'Speaking of which, I am now going off to make the good May laugh.'

'I don't think she feels much like laughing today.'

'She say anything to you about the cheques business? Doesn't matter. All a misunderstanding. You'll see. I'll be . . .' and he hesitated, '*nice* to her'; offering the word with a wink and a nod, only too pleased to share it with her.

Later, from behind the closed door she heard his voice murmur and May Stewart mingle her laughter with his like a betrayal so that she could have wept at how alone she was.

13

'What made you think Professor Ure would be here today? I mean, today of all days!'

In the empty concrete corridor, Sam Wilson's question waited echoing on its answer. Through one of the glass panels which made up the outer wall, Sophie watched the stand of birches by the loch scratch their stripped branches against the clouds. Grey yet luminous, the light threatened snow before dark. She had written to Maitland at home, something he had forbidden her ever to do; but though she had stayed off work and waited in her room he had not come. Last night it had been his wife who answered the phone, but she had babbled something about the Trust and then there had been the sound of his voice. She stared at the bruised sky and wished Wilson would go away. She did not want him there when Maitland came.

'The students have *gone*.' Little Sam, Maitland called him; though she was not tall for a woman, he had to look up to her. As if to make up for this, his emphatic speech with its unexpected stresses made a claim to be regarded. 'Students and so *staff*, naturally. Numbers of my colleagues, as always, beat all but the nimblest of our clients out of the door. But all of them are gone now – gone where the *good* family men go.'

He laughed too much, looked at her breasts and glanced away.

'Family men?'

'Today of all days. Surely tonight's the one for hanging up stockings and all that sort of thing.'

It was Christmas Eve. She had insisted that Maitland meet her on Christmas Eve.

'I think he has to come in for something,' she said.

'To see you?'

'Oh, no!' As if her mind was in compartments, the denial was natural and unforced. It would be absurd for Professor Ure to come in specially to see an ex-student – and on Christmas Eve 'of all days'.

'But why then, I wonder . . .'

'For – something else. But it means he can see me here.'

'All this way,' Wilson said. 'Didn't you say you were working in Edinburgh now? Did you come by car?'

'I got the train.'

'To the station in Balinter?'

She nodded.

'And then did you walk? From the station in Balinter? But it's miles!'

'It didn't seem far,' she said.

'You must want to see Professor Ure very *badly*.'

She thought about that, then said, 'I would have been coming anyway. To visit friends. I'm going to stay with a friend.'

'Who would that be? If it's someone from your time here, I dare say I'll know her.'

It was hot in the corridor. Despite all the talk about economies, the central heating was on and set high. The heavy dryness stifled her. She stared out at the chill angular landscape, willing him to leave her alone.

'It's business,' she said, as she had explained to Lucy Ure. 'I work for the Trust—'

'The Gregory and Rintoul. Of course. I'd been told you went there. It's the Professor's pet charity.'

Did he tell you? she wanted to ask. She hungered after the idea that Maitland could not resist speaking of her.

'We take an interest in our old students – our ex-students.' He smiled. 'Of course, you know you were one of my disappointments.'

She felt the word superstitiously, that he should use it like an omen while she waited for Maitland to come.

'I recognised you at once. When I saw you standing here, I said to myself, But that's Sophie Lindgren who I was so sure was going to do honours. It's a let-down when people don't *do* all you hoped they might.'

She had won a class prize in the summer; and after that she had fallen in love with Maitland.

'I don't have any regrets,' she said.

'Early days,' but he smiled, which made it only a joke. 'So you've come all this way on behalf of the Trust. It's terribly conscientious of you.'

'It's something that has to be decided at once.' Her father would say good lies are built out of as much of the truth as you can use. 'The Trust is taking a party of patients to the theatre as a holiday treat. It happens every year apparently.'

'And something's come up? You have an emergency?'

'Patients from the hospital the original Gregory worked in,' she offered as if that was an answer.

'He was a surgeon,' he said, having the academic's requirement to share what he knew.

'It's a different kind of hospital now. Professor Ure's father-in-law worked there as a psychiatrist.'

'And do you go with them? As *part* of your duties?'

'They have helpers. People volunteer. But, yes, I'll be going. The secretary, Mrs Stewart, is very keen. It's not like a job to her – more like a . . .'

'Vocation,' he finished for her. A boy in her seminar group when he had a paper to read hesitated so often and so skilfully that Wilson plugged every gap in his preparation, and never seemed to notice. 'All the same – the holiday season – I shouldn't think she could insist on your going.'

'I don't mind. I expect it'll be enormous fun.'

'Wonderful to be young,' he said, and she thought he was laughing at her. In her own ears, her foolish voice rang bright, enormously bright. 'Life begins at forty. Isn't

102

that what they say?' As if it could matter to her what age he was, the little pompous creature. 'As a new arrival, I'm perfectly willing to find it so.'

She stared out to the curve of road above the loch where a car would first come into sight.

'. . . Perhaps you're here to persuade Professure Ure?'

'Persuade him?'

But that was too shrill. He looked at her shrewdly. 'To go on your theatrical outing. Where are you taking them – for entertainment – your *unfortunates*?'

'This year it's to be the Palace.'

'That great barn! Isn't it used now only for pop concerts? All those young things squealing and getting themselves *over*excited. Would your sick enjoy that kind of thing?'

Would Maitland never come? She forced herself to find something to say. 'It's very seasonal. Not a pop concert. A kind of variety show – singers, jugglers, a comedian, I suppose. The second half of the show is all the Great Sovek. It was that or a pantomime – and they voted for a change.'

He shook his head. 'You'll never persuade him. I'd give up if I was you. Professor Ure and the *Great* Sovek – not forgetting the jugglers, and a comedian, you suppose!'

It could only be by accident he sounded sardonic. Everyone knew he hero-worshipped Maitland.

'But he does go! . . . So Mrs Stewart tells me.'

'It'll be because of his wife. People who live in villages tend to develop the Lady Bountiful thing. You know they live in a village? – lovely view of the hills.' Without altering his tone, he went on, 'You're having a long wait. Perhaps he isn't going to come.'

As he said this, he checked the time, not by glancing at his wristwatch or turning to look at the clock on the wall, but by looking up to where its image was reflected in the glass against the darkening sky. As she followed his gaze, the minute hand tugged forward as if to pull her bound by the wrists towards whatever was in wait for her.

'I can't see that he's going to come now,' Sam Wilson said, and she was ready to believe him except that like a burly miracle a thick-set man in the grey uniform of the security staff appeared. 'Miss Lindgren? . . . I was asked to check if you were still here. Professor Ure sends his apologies for being so late. He is on his way.'

'I was on the point of offering you a coffee,' Sam Wilson said. 'Or something stronger – with it being the festive season.'

'There wouldn't be time, not since he is coming.'

'Well, yes, I had seen that. Perhaps another day.'

They stood in silence. She wondered why he did not go. She needed time to prepare herself.

'I have a flat in the residences. But perhaps you knew that?'

'No.'

'Rent-free. It's one of the perks of being an academic warden. Normally the place is full of life and I like that. Being around young people, it's never dull.' His voice had quietened and lost its odd emphatic stresses. 'But now, of course, they've all gone home.'

As a student she had lived in one of the residences, and had a picture of him offering her coffee in a room like that; her on the seat by the desk and him cross-legged on the bed. She wanted to share the joke with someone, with Maitland if only he would come.

'Do you keep up?'

'Sorry?' What was he talking about now?

'With the subject. Do you take an interest still at all?'

Didn't he know that even those with honours degrees were counting themselves lucky to find jobs in sales or personnel? It was a different world from the one into which he had graduated. His question irritated her beyond reason. Did he think she should 'keep up' as a hobby? Or for love?

When he began talking of Maitland's attitude to the students, it was worse because she had to hide her anger, having no right to it.

It seemed to her a long time before the beams of a car, tilted by the crest of the ascent, raked like searchlights across the dark. When Maitland appeared, he came from the wrong end of the corridor, catching her by surprise.

'You've missed Dr Wilson.'

'Good.'

'I couldn't get rid of him. When we saw your car, he went off towards the front door. But you came the other way.'

'We don't want to stand here,' Maitland said. 'It's like a bloody fishbowl.'

Hurrying after him, she realised he must have seen Wilson standing with her as he got out of his car. She wondered if that was why he had chosen to come in by the other door. Breathlessly, she said, 'I was angry with him. He was criticising you.'

Maitland grunted without looking back.

'He thinks you upset the students by wondering if any of it matters. He can't understand why you do it.'

The truth was that Wilson had surprised her by the strength of his feeling. 'I know,' he had said, 'that he's only . . . joking. That's not the right word either. He wants to challenge them into thinking about the value of what we do. But they misunderstand. They come to me and I tell them, Christ, the Professor's played his part – he's worked with everybody in the field who matters. It's all *to do*. There's *plenty* to do, I tell them.' In his seminars, when she was a student, he had never conveyed to her, to any of them, this simple truth – that he was in love with his subject. 'The terrible thing is,' he said, a little patch of colour on each cheek, 'that it's the brightest students who are most unsettled by him.'

Now, as she followed him into his office, Maitland asked, 'Did you want me to meet you so we could discuss Wilson's opinion of how I handle students?'

'Did you know,' she responded, 'I've just realised you don't ever talk to me about any of that. You tell me what Wilson or Black are getting up to – or how McBain isn't much better than a Government stooge for the next round of cuts. That's only gossip. You don't share what you're doing with me – not your real work.'

'My "real work".' He settled on the edge of the desk, unbuttoning his coat one-handed. The heavy cloth slid open over his thighs. His skin had the healthy look of a man who spent time out of doors. There were lines at the corners of his eyes, but with his brown skin and thick curling black hair he looked like a man in his thirties. 'It's not a particularly obvious topic between lovers.'

'We could talk.' She knew she was making herself vulnerable and silly, but could not stop. 'I have a degree. I try to keep up.'

'Below a certain level,' he said, 'shop talk doesn't interest me.'

Tears stung her eyes, although she knew he had not meant to be cruel. He meant no more than what he had said and, if she had drawn it out of him, then it was by her own foolishness. Unexpectedly, horribly, she heard herself asking, 'Can you talk to your wife? I suppose she'd understand more of it?'

'She used to,' he said coolly. 'She's out of touch now.'

She could not believe she had got herself into this mess. She had been kept waiting too long for him.

'You said you'd be here hours ago. I was so afraid you weren't going to come.' It seemed whatever was in her head had to be blurted out. She had to control herself. 'It's just that you were so late.'

'I always had this image of you as being placid,' he said. 'It was one of the things I liked about you.'

A swimmer going into cold water, she took her breath deeply. 'Did you know your wife was at the flat? With Monty Norman? I saw her there.'

He stared impassively.

Said at last, 'If you feel you must, tell me.'

'It was in the afternoon. I had gone home . . .'

*

Home is the safest place for weeping. People called it home where for a time they slept; even in a dreary room in a flat whispering with strangers. Real home for Sophie would have meant a train journey north, except that she would have felt it unfair to cry in front of her father. He had worked so hard to climb up out of the need for tears. It was a battle which he had been obliged to win, since the ones who did not had a high casualty rate. In charge at last of the company's sales team, he made a habit of retailing the mishaps of this changing cast to his family. Unpromoted salesmen were the walking wounded. Men she would never meet limped out of the memories of her earliest childhood: men with stomach complaints, men weeping on corners or found hallucinating in the bedrooms of small-town hotels. Their stories told over the dinner-table had been offered by her father to his family like guarantees of safety. His battle won, that table was the last place in the world to which she could bring her tears.

At this time of the afternoon, the flat would be empty; everyone had a job except the Irish boy who wanted to be a painter, and lately he had begun to let them all know that he found his room, which he used as a studio, too depressing to be alone in during the day. The corridor was dusky; the only light struggled through the transom windows above two of the bedroom doors. She stepped heavy-limbed and slow as if under water through the twilight dimness. Her room was a cave full of shadows. Winter light pressed like grey water against the single window. In another week it would be Christmas. She huddled her coat around her and stared unseeing at the brown and grey cones of the unlit gas fire. Nothing here belonged to her: not the lumpy chair, or the scratched dressing-table, or the wardrobe with the piece of folded cardboard pushed in under the door to keep it from swinging open; not the bed, above which she had tacked up when she took possession in the summer a poster of the Théâtre Molière – Le Théâtre Gai de la Porte de Namur. She had taken it down after Maitland made a joke about student digs. He had meant no harm but it was not the way she wanted hm to think of her, and anyway she had only put it up because the wallpaper was so drab. This was the place where Maitland belonged to her and to no one else in the world. This was her true and only home.

She touched the blank place where the Théâtre Molière and its comfort of bright colours had shone down on her in Maitland's arms. Months ago she had folded it into a bin sack in the kitchen and then, for fear anyone should ask her why, poured rubbish on to hide it from view. It had been warm then on summer afternoons, and thinking of how it had been she went restlessly into the hall. From beyond the door of his room, which was not quite shut, came the deep measured note of Monty Norman's voice. Horribly startled as if she had been spied on, she stood with her fingers pressed across her lips listening.

'Down on his knees digging into her, made me laugh. Many's the laugh I've had with Georgie. I wonder what they did to him. Too fat to run away – poor bloody Georgie.'

His voice came and went and there was the tramp of his feet as he moved about the room. She pushed at the door, just with one finger gently so that she could peep inside; impulsively, out of the silly feeling he had no right to be there.

Back to her he was talking to himself, leaning forward with both hands on the iron rail at the end of the bed.

'Georgie brought it on himself. Brought that young bastard in without a by your leave. Even so, who's to say Georgie Clarke isn't the lucky one? He's not stuck in this hole. What do you say? you say nothing, bloody nothing—'

And on the last word, a little explosion of anger, he had pushed himself upright – and she glimpsed the bed and recognised the woman lying outstretched on it. Seeing Sophie, his face loosened with astonishment and then with

108

a shrug he said, 'I'm complaining about having to live in this dump.'

Although there was no hysteria in her laughter but a rich easiness of relief, she could not stop even when she discovered that Monty Norman had followed her back into her room.

'Was there something you wanted?'

At the ridiculous politeness of his question the laughter welled up filling her mouth and spilling out in bright shards.

'I think you've made a mistake,' he said.

She remembered his terrible contained anger in the bar when the reporter woman – what was her name? what was her name? – had humiliated him. Maitland had thought it funny when she told him. He had not seen Norman's anger or how his hand holding the glass had trembled. But still the laughter came, thinner and metallic with the taste of fear.

'Come and see,' he said, and walked away not doubting that she would follow.

She had not expected Lucy Ure still to be lying on the bed. It was as if she had intruded upon an act of death not sex. But the murderer said, 'I'm glad you've stopped laughing. I was beginning to worry about you.'

'What have you done to her? Is she drugged?'

He gave an odd snorting grunt of amusement. 'What an imagination you have!'

'Her eyes are open, but she's not looking. What's wrong with her?'

'No drugs,' Monty Norman said. 'Lucy, get up and make yourself comfortable in the chair ... You see? She can hear. She moves. After all, there's nothing terrible happening.'

Yet to Sophie there was something unnatural in her rising so responsively and in the manner of her sitting, upright but flopped and slack in the shoulders.

'Mrs Ure?' she asked hesitantly. 'You said she could hear – but she doesn't!'

He turned his glance from one woman to the other.

'You know Professor Ure's wife is not well?'

'No. I never heard anyone say that.'

'Of course, there's no reason why you should know.' He paused, and she made a movement of her head as if to agree. 'Have you been to their home?'

She shook her head again. She had no reason to go; no reason. It was as if he was taunting her with her exclusion from Maitland's life.

'While I was there, she became unwell. Do you know anything about migraine? Don't compare it to what happens when you get a bad headache. It's real pain. People who get it when they're driving, have to pull in at the side of the road. It blinds them. She's a bad case. She hates it and it frightens her. The attacks have been coming more often lately. She comes to me because I can help her.'

'Help her?'

'Go up to her. Closer. Do you understand?'

'Her eyes are open, but she doesn't see me. Mrs Ure?'

She stretched out her hand to touch the older woman on the cheek, then drew it back, partly in fright, more from a sudden sense of shame.

'She felt an attack coming on – they get a kind of warning, you see. And, luckily, she was nearby. She's under hypnosis. I've helped other people – and I'm trying to help her. It's something I can do, but I don't talk about it. It's not something I want to be known for – either people would pester me and make it cheap like a party trick, or they'd be begging for me to help them. I'd get no peace. I can't help everyone, and I wouldn't charge for it – not when it's a gift.'

If he was telling the truth, he was taking back from her that wonderful chance: to free Maitland from his marriage – and not be blamed. It was too unfair. Yet his confidence confused her. If the story was crazy, its best witness was Lucy Ure, so blank-eyed and oblivious.

At the same time, like a deep cut saving its hurt for later, she began the process of understanding that, if it

110

was true, Maitland had told her nothing about his wife's illness. If that part of his life meant anything to him, he had shut her out.

The snap of his fingers jerked her attention back. 'I thought you were gone.' He clicked his fingers again, lightly, smiling at her. 'After all nothing so terrible. She's sick and I help her. I don't blame you for wondering what was going on. She's ill and now she's well. She's happy.' Deep and pleasant, his voice was the only unusual thing about him. 'Why shouldn't you be happy too? Why not, eh? She'll wake up in a minute and be on top of the world. Look here, why don't you sit down? For a minute. You've had a bit of excitement. Why not rest for a bit?'

'Does Maitland know what is going on?' she asked.

'No,' he said sharply, his tone quite different. 'Mrs Ure prefers that her husband shouldn't know. Some men don't like to share the power they have over their wives. The idea of hypnotism upsets them. They don't understand it's only medicine. It's like getting upset because their wife takes aspirin. It makes life simpler if they don't know.'

'Are you going to waken her?'

'She'll waken when it's time.'

'If you woke her now, she could tell me herself. That she doesn't want Maitland to know.'

'The treatment isn't complete. It isn't time to waken her.'

'You could put her back to sleep afterwards.'

'It doesn't occur to you she would be embarrassed? Waking up to find a stranger here?'

Her breath came chokingly, as if the exchange had been with swords not words.

'Not a complete stranger,' she said. 'And next time I see her I'll ask her about these migraines.'

When he smiled, it changed his face which in repose was fleshy and slightly coarse. The thickness, the curliness, the very definite black of his hair gave a kind of expectation of handsomeness which although not really there would impose on some women. He was not Sophie's type.

111

If she had been asked, she would have explained that by saying she preferred her men to look more intelligent. The way then in which this smile changed him disconcerted her. It lightened the load of flesh with a momentary illumination; and if it was a showman's charm, still it was charm.

It was with this smile, he asked her, 'Will you tell her at the same time why you call her husband by his first name? "Maitland" – you say it so naturally. Are you going to explain to her why that is?'

'Are you?' Maitland wondered.

Yes. Sooner or later, somehow. Had Monty Norman thought he was being clever? She had wanted to say to him, Wake her up! Let's tell her now who I am and what I mean to Maitland!

'Haven't I the right to be happy?' Unexamined, the appeal burst from her and broke upon his look of incomprehension. Trembling, she went on, 'You know I wouldn't.'

'So what happened?'

'That was all. I went back to my room. I sat on the bed. After a while, the outer door closed.'

'You expect me to believe this?'

She stared at him in shock. One hand reached out palm upward, longing to be held.

Haven't I the right to be happy? Her question was a tremor of the air which separated them.

'I never pretended to you that I wanted to change my life.' In his bulky expensive coat, he rested on the edge of the desk like a rock, heavy and solid with darkness. 'I didn't think I had to put it into words. If I should have done, then I'm sorry.'

For a rock, it was a handsome apology. Rock sins necessarily being sins of omission.

'Are you being cruel to be kind, Maitland?' she whispered, hardly knowing what she was saying. 'Is that what

112

you think you have to do? My father talks about being cruel to be kind.'

'Neither the one nor the other,' he said, who had been so kind in the wordless sliding promises of his flesh in hers. 'Just realistic. You can't change one kind of relationship into another, Sophie, just by wishing. You weren't content with what we had – you wanted to change things. Well, that's what you've done. You've made it impossible for us.'

'Your wonderful marriage,' she said. Her lips were numb as if after a beating. 'It's Christmas Eve. You should be at home hanging up stockings for the children. Only there aren't any. She hasn't given you any, has she?'

'This isn't doing either of us a bit of good.' He turned at the door, one hand resting on the handle, no more than pausing in the act of leaving. 'One thing. If you did tell my wife we'd been to bed together – if you couldn't stop yourself doing that – it would distress her and infuriate me. But it wouldn't alter anything. Be a sensible girl.'

She sat at his desk and touched the things gently that lay on its surface. Only now did it occur to her that she should have asked Maitland if his wife suffered from migraine. Whatever she picked up, she was careful to set down in the same place. Nothing was disarranged. If Lucy Ure was ill, couldn't he see that proved she was telling the truth? Except that someone else might have told her about his wife being ill. Wasn't that what he would think? There was an executive toy perhaps given to him by some colleague as a joke: the dolphin, drawn back and released, rocked back and forward through a hoop. No matter how far back you took it or how often you tried, it would never rock free.

The door was thrown open. A man stood there with one hand up as if ready for self-defence.

'God, it's you,' he said. 'I didn't know who it was when I saw the light.'

She recognised the security guard who had told her Maitland would come.

'Professor Ure phoned from home that he'd forgotten to lock his door,' the man said. 'All these doors have to be kept locked.'

'It's all right.' She got up from behind the desk. 'I haven't touched anything.'

Unexpectedly, at that he grinned. He had a flat face, brick red from the open air, and he grinned as if she had said something dirty.

Sam Wilson had warned her, watching the lights of Maitland's car claw the dark sky.

'Don't – try not to take things too seriously, Miss Lindgren. You're not the *first*, you know. You have your whole life in front of you. That's precious. Don't let it be spoiled.' Stopped then, staggered by his own daring, to blink and finish weakly. 'We've all been young and had our problems.'

He had stared so solemnly, trying to hold her gaze – her eyes hungry to be done with him – willing her to understand without the risk of putting more into words. What he said meant nothing to her then, and she was glad when he chose to go, hurrying away along the grey corridors in the wrong direction for meeting Maitland.

BOOK FOUR

The Great Sovek

14

When the Great Sovek threw back his head and laughed, Lucy was standing too close to him so that she saw his tongue and the inside of his mouth very red against the black frame of his beard. The impression stayed with her unpleasantly so that when later from the audience she watched him come on to the stage, against a background of black drapes and red curtains looped back at the sides, the red of the proscenium arch flecked with golden paint, it was as if he stood in an open mouth. Like a golden tooth, he glittered out at her from the open mouth of the stage.

But that was later. Now, caught in the spiced outflow of his breath, she tried to step aside, but he held her still by the hand.

'Nervous? No, I like to have company. I leave nerves to the fat comedian, whom you're having the good taste to give a miss.'

Truth was, she would have liked to hear the comedian, and there would be singers, perhaps a juggler, people like that. It was Maitland who, having no patience for such things, had initiated this visit backstage.

'Tell us though when you would like us to leave,' Maitland said. 'I imagine you must want time to yourself before you go on.'

'I have no nerves,' the Great Sovek reaffirmed, letting go of her hand and laughing widely as if to share with them his delight in himself.

The greenroom was crowded with the privileged who

had come behind the scenes and along the dusty little corridor to where the hypnotist was passing the time until the second half, his half, of the show should begin. Behind her, Lucy heard the soft rising note of the undulant young man who had shown them the way. 'Oh, reading it's all very well, but it isn't the play. I mean it was extraordinary. Everyone who was there speaks of it in such a special manner. We're like a club – we say to one another, Yes, I saw him that night and it was magical, such a performance.'

She wondered if he could be speaking of the hypnotist, but then a woman's voice said something about Shakespeare and she realised that if he was stagestruck it was not for the kind of performance they might expect from the Great Sovek. The woman's voice was soft with a different lilt to it so that it was easy to lose some of the words. When she spoke again, Lucy glanced behind and saw that it was one of the two women who had come from the hospital as part of the patients' escort, a pale heavy-featured girl with dark hair tightly pulled back and large unsuitable glasses. Meeting her glance, the girl smiled.

'Shouldn't you be with your patients?' Lucy asked.

Instead of answering, the girl made a face, pulling her lips together and raising heavy brows above the glasses' frame. It might have meant anything. Yes. No. Mind your own business, I'm having fun. Anything. But when, giving up, Lucy turned from the girl, she faced into a silence. People were looking at her. Sophie Lindgren was looking at her.

'If I were liable to nerves,' the Great Sovek said, frowning around to lay claim to all of their attention, 'there wouldn't be any performance. I have to be confident – how else would I impose my will on others?'

'Is that what you do?' Maitland wondered. 'It sounds ugly. Wouldn't you say it sounds ugly?'

Appealed to, Monty Norman shrugged. 'It's a bit of fun, isn't it?'

'Entertainment, you mean?'

'I put on a show,' the Great Sovek said. Some of his vowels he spoke through his nose so that Lucy wondered if he might be American – or Canadian? 'People have a good time. They go out smiling.'

'Couldn't the fat comedian say as much?' Maitland asked.

When he took someone up in that way, it was because his interest was caught. He paid them the compliment of every scrap of his attention. She had been disturbed to hear someone – Sam Wilson? yes, at some gathering of the faculty – a voice behind her saying, 'Maitland being aggressive again.' The tone warm, affectionate, anticipatory, but to her it still seemed like a criticism. And one which wasn't true. They didn't understand the eagerness of his mind. In all the years, he hadn't changed in that; he hadn't changed. And she should have told him Sophie Lindgren's story, all of it, the invention of a sick girl. The sensible thing would have been to tell him (I've had the strangest experience . . . And then she said . . . Something will have to be done about her); but she had not been able to bring herself to do it. The whole thing was too shameful. Yet she should have told him. The girl was dangerous.

'You haven't heard his jokes!' the Great Sovek cried, and there was a flurry of laughter which startled her. Monty Norman was laughing loudly with his mouth open like a man calling for help. May Stewart, on the other hand, and the man Terence, the one who had just written his thesis funded by the Trust, made a narrow grin of their mouths as if afraid too much might escape; both of them with their eyes fixed on Maitland as if for permission. I hope at least he's paid for his own ticket, she thought; it would be disgraceful if the Trust has paid for his ticket. And thinking of nothing else, concentrated on thinking of nothing else, she looked at Sophie Lindgren who stared back as unsmiling as herself.

'To come back to the idea of will-power, though. Is

119

there much need after all for that commodity, I wonder?'
Dull Mr Terence with his mouth making scholarly distinctions while his eyes checked with Maitland to see if this was an acceptable line to pursue. He knows which side his bread is buttered on, Lucy thought.

'You think not?'

'It seems a possibility that the ones who "go under" – would that be the right way to put it? – lack the power of resistance, don't have much will of their own to be overpowered.'

'Easy meat, you mean?' The Great Sovek bared square white teeth as credentials for his power to chew.

'I couldn't see myself going under. I'm not the type.'

'I don't take on challenges.' At the admission, Mr Terence nodded as if to say, Just as well in *this* case. 'I used to, but it isn't wise. When I was younger, I did. One time the guy feeling himself go started lashing out. With his fists. I hadn't realised he was so afraid.'

'And did you succeed?'

'Oh, yes. But I got a black eye for my trouble.'

Again there was a response startling Lucy by its strangeness, making her feel all of them were uncomfortable with this talk of submission, of going under, a metaphor for drowning. Why else would they produce these sounds not like real laughter, like a mimicry of laughter? She bent her head under a flurry of barks and whinnyings, soft expulsions and braying like the clatter of metallic parts.

'What do you make these people do?' Lucy heard herself ask.

Perhaps she had spoken too loudly or too abruptly; or perhaps only that it was unexpected, coming without any preparation. It made a silence.

'I shan't spoil it.' The Great Sovek shot a cuff to consult a wafer of gold strapped to the inside of his wrist. 'Not long to go, then you'll see for yourself.'

'What? I can't imagine *what*.'

He stared at her as if suddenly offended. 'You needn't worry. No one is made a fool of in my show. People have the wrong idea. I work in hospitals. Doctors ask my advice.'

'You spoke of making others submit to your will,' Maitland said.

'There's a power involved. That's one way of describing it.'

'Isn't power something that lends itself to being abused?'

'It doesn't work like that. Listen. If I told a young girl on the stage – Take off your clothes! What do you think would happen?' He looked from one man to the other around the circle, gauging each reaction in turn. Laughed. 'She'd wake up!'

'So it's all a sham.'

'I don't know that word.'

'A kind of game. They are pretending.'

'It's not *like* that. How would you go about pretending not to feel pain while a knife was cutting you open?' He drew a line with his finger across his stomach and then added in case of misunderstanding, 'Like I said, hospitals. At home in Toronto there's a doctor I work with.'

'Ah, then, if it's a game,' Maitland said with the graceful air of a man conceding a point, 'it's a serious one.'

No one realised about the man in the corner until he reacted to the *bersagliere* story.

The Great Sovek told it. 'I heard it when I was in Italy. They say a lawyer in Palermo was defending a guy against a charge of rape. He went up to one of the *bersagliere*, the soldiers on guard in the court, you know those guys with the long feather in their hats? – I don't know, maybe this was a while ago – anyway, the guy is wearing a sword. So the lawyer gets him to take it out, and the lawyer takes the scabbard. Put your sword back in the scabbard, the lawyer says. And the guy tries, but he can't manage it. Slip your sword in! Slide your sword into its place! the lawyer encourages him. By this time the soldier is sweating, he's embarrassed, everybody is laughing. He's trying, but he can't manage it. Why?' The Great Sovek mimed with his hand, 'Because the lawyer is doing this – just moving the end of the scabbard a little back a little forward.' He grinned round at all of them. 'The guy was acquitted. Not guilty!'

Lucy did not see the point of the story or what connection it had with anything said before. Some people were smiling, however; and then the man in the corner, a very ordinary man with a fat pale face, the jacket of his suit too tight for him, not anyone you would notice, cried out, 'He should have put the sword to his throat!' He came forward to where the Great Sovek was lolling back in his seat, and gestured to him, 'You do it – the scabbard, yes, see, like that,' and the hypnotist held up his hand as instructed. 'I'm trying to put the sword in – and you're – that's right, moving it,' and he held out his empty fist at arm's length trying to match the wavering of the hypnotist's hand. 'But now!' and with the word, he moved his arm up until it pointed not at the hypnotist's throat but at his face and Lucy saw the sword there, the light running along its length, so that eased forward only a fraction it would plunge into the soft eye. 'Not a muscle, right? Don't risk it. Keep still.' And slowly he lowered his fist and edged it forward straight-armed until the edge of it knocked at last with a small sucking sound against the palm of the Great Sovek's outstretched hand.

'In up to the hilt,' he said. 'Guilty.'

Lucy who had visited the hospital a long time ago when her father was alive and walked with him through the wards – 'Don't be afraid, child,' he whispered, the smell and warmth of his cheek beside her own – guessed at once; but most of the people probably didn't realise what was wrong until the pale girl with the glasses – covering half her face, like goggles, making her look stupid, anything to be in fashion – took him by the arm and led him from the room.

Even then some of them didn't understand, and it was against the bright fluttering of explanations, relief, someone was laughing, 'Who was hypnotised that time?' at the Great Sovek who scowled, that she said to Maitland, 'He should have been kept with the others. He should never have been here. Or the girl either.'

He looked at her for a speculative moment, and then turned away.

She touched him on the arm. 'You should speak to the doctor.'

'She is the doctor,' he said, and began to speak to someone else.

Instead of going back to their seats, they went to the bar to spend the interval and she was more or less part of a group that seemed to be talking about Christmas and the undulant young man said, 'But who carried the flesh and wine – not to mention the bloody pine logs? Oh, yes, he was good, Wenceslas's page might have admitted, but only good as *kings* go' and the laughter spiralled up and drifted back with the thin smoke – people didn't smoke so much, not any more, not in public, she'd noticed that – and she held her headache at a distance like something ugly that might be a mistake and not there at all if only you could avoid looking full at it, keeping it in the corner of your eye. 'Are you all right?' Monty Norman asked, and she went right away across the room without answering him which must have seemed rude. When she dared to look back, he was talking with a sharp-faced older woman, who stared up at him putting strays of hair back from her forehead. She wasn't sure and then she was – It's Viv Law, for she had met the journalist, though just once or twice and not recently, and anyway she was exactly as Sophie Lindgren had described her.

That liar.

All the time with one part of her she had wanted to confront the girl. Now she had to fight the urge to pull her away from where she stood in the circle around Maitland and drag her over beside Viv Law and Monty Norman. Look! she would say to her, no trembling hands, no hate, just two people talking together, normal people, not sick things out of a nightmare.

What a scene that would be! How would she explain it

to Maitland? Poor darling, he would wonder what was going on. He would have no idea. She saw Mr Terence nodding at her as if to share the joke and realised she had joined in the laughter.

Maitland held their tickets in his left hand, glancing at them and then at the white letter painted on the end of each row; yet behind him Lucy had no difficulty in seeing where they must be going. The heavy-featured girl, the one Maitland had said was the doctor, from an aisle seat halfway down on the right was twisted round watching them.

We're going to have to squeeze in past her, Lucy thought, and then by the patients – they were all there, probably they had remained seated all through the interval, that would have been best (unless they had wanted to go to the toilet? that would be why there would be two nurses, the male one she had mistaken for the doctor) – it was unpleasant to think of having to touch them, feel the pressure of their knees, bodies, would they realise they should stand up to let people pass? worse almost if they did stand up. Then Maitland was stopping, leaning down to exchange words with the doctor, and there were two empty seats in the row just behind, and she was ashamed of what she had been thinking and busy with that she had sat down before realising the woman in the next seat was Sophie Lindgren.

Before she could react, Maitland had taken his place beside her, still talking to the doctor woman. A hand touched her lightly on the shoulder. From the row behind, Monty Norman's face was pushed towards hers.

'It's all right now?' he asked. 'The professor's wife suffers from headaches,' he explained to Sophie Lindgren.

Nothing could have been more reasonably sympathetic than his tone, but Sophie Lindgren shrank from him. The movement was so exaggerated that Lucy knew the girl had to be acting.

Monty Norman eased back until he was framed between May Stewart and cautious Mr Terence seated on either side of him, just where he should be, in the context of the Trust for which he worked, nothing could be more normal.

'It's kind of you to ask.' She felt a sudden warmth towards the little vulgar good-hearted man. 'You're quite right, I wasn't feeling well. But I feel better now.'

'It was the heat in the bar, I expect.'

'And the noise.'

He leaned forward again. 'Are you looking forward to the show?'

'I'm not sure.'

'Me neither. It's not my cup of tea, not what I'd pay to go and see, not left to myself. – Would you?' but Sophie Lindgren seemed not to hear him.

It was nearly time, most of the audience were seated, in a moment the lights would dim.

The patient in front of her, the man who had been led out of the greenroom, was sitting with his head bent forward. He's crying, she thought, while that wretched girl ignores him, not caring. What kind of doctor does she call herself? A wave of indignation swept over her, but when she leaned forward in protest to comfort him he was bent over an ice-cream rubbing it with his lips and sucking pieces into his mouth.

As she sank back feeling slightly sick, the auditorium darkened and the Great Sovek was there alone on stage, appearing from nowhere it seemed in an outflowing of Indian-sounding music. He asked them to clasp their fingers, intertwine them, tighter and tighter; but when she went to do so Maitland laid his hand gently over hers. It was just as well since next they were told that it might be hard to separate their hands, and almost at once people were shuffling along the rows, crouched in embarrassment or grinning towards the stage. She felt a touch on her arm and it was Sophie Lindgren, pressing against her with hands clasped tightly together. She pulled away in disgust but the girl leaned towards her. Her lips came close almost touching Lucy's cheek. Thinking about it afterwards, she knew it must have been noisy, yet she never doubted that it was then she heard Sophie Lindgren sigh.

The girl's head fell forward.

But then she was on her feet and pushing past them into the passage.

'Something's wrong,' Lucy said. 'Something's wrong with her.'

Maitland paid no attention, smiling to himself as he watched the trickle of people mounting the steps. The Great Sovek met them there, releasing their hands with a touch and sending some back down to join the audience and others, Sophie among them, to a row of seats set out in the centre of the stage.

Such a strange sigh the girl had given.

It was done so quickly. No pendulums or swinging watches, 'Look into my eyes'; none of that. Lucy had never seen anyone being hypnotised except in old films, and then it was only actors pretending. The Great Sovek walked behind the line of seated people, touching each one on the neck; he hardly paused and yet each time the head fell forward as if in sleep. Perhaps if he were slower, they would realise what was about to happen and jump up. It would spoil things if too many of them did that. They were being given no time to change their minds.

Sophie Lindgren was near the end of the row on the right, or on the left – wasn't that so? for the people up there it would be on the left; stage left. How still she sat, her hands in her lap and her head bent forward. But they were all like that, almost all of them; she was no different from the others. And there were as many men as women. She had taken it for granted that men would be better able to resist. All of them were young, of course; and she thought that might be why, and then wondered if older people had gone up and been rejected. She hadn't noticed because she had been watching Sophie Lindgren. Someone with white hair sitting up there in that row of dreamers would be not entertaining but sad.

Strange that none of the patients had tried to go up. If

one of them had tried, she hadn't noticed. Yet if weakness of will was involved – but, of course, the nurses would have stopped them. The girl doctor perhaps had stretched out to her neighbour, putting her hand over his as a warning, stopping him from whatever risk there might be in finding he couldn't unclasp his fingers. The Great Sovek might have had more than he bargained for. But then part of his skill must lie in not choosing—

I don't degrade anyone in my act, the Great Sovek had said in the greenroom – *not the young man who was proposing marriage down on one knee pleading with an empty chair?* They uncover abilities they never knew they had, that's what it's about – *like the girl eating the lemon now and wiping the sweet juice from her chin?* People who can't sing sing, guys with two left feet dance the tango – *and the man having a bath with all his clothes on?* It was only fun, she was being ridiculous, it was part of a show, no different from the comedian, singer, juggler. Listen to them laugh.

She hated what was happening on stage.

The patients from the unit for the depressed, the addicted, the disoriented, seemed to be laughing in the right places. They leaned forward, cried out; in the blurred dark, they were no different from the rest of the audience. As if he had read her thoughts, the man who had been eating the ice-cream turned round and smiled at her – traces of sticky stuff dry around his mouth. She was in pain. Without warning or preparation, pain ran like acid behind her eyes.

The hypnotist's performance was moving to its climax. For this, everyone had to be involved. The stage began to fill with figures. A boy of about twenty sat up and begged with hanging paws, fell down on all fours again, yapped and cocked up a leg – sobs of laughter. Like a circus clown spinning plates, the Great Sovek hurried back and forward. He spoke to the two men gyrating together and they *were* dancing the tango. He drew up his puppets slack-jointed and gave them worlds of their own. The row of chairs was almost empty. He had touched Sophie and then moved on, come back to her quickly and then turned to someone else. Now the boy on all fours came sidling sideways like a mongrel. Boydog he sniffed at Sophie Lindgren's spread legs.

People sometimes pretended to be hypnotised. Said afterwards it was a joke. The boy moved his face up along the inside of her leg.

It was only when Maitland caught at her that Lucy realised she had got to her feet. 'It's wrong,' she said to him. He pulled at her to make her sit down. The hypnotist was standing looking at what was happening, not stopping it. Laughter rolled forward like a wave that would knock her from her feet. In the row behind they were shouting at her to sit down. Sophie Lindgren was slipping down in her chair, the boy's head was hidden by her skirt, her legs sprawled open. The hypnotist came forward at last and bent over her. It was indecent.

'Can't you see she's dead?' she screamed.

It wasn't what she had intended to say; but as the Great Sovek straightened and turned with his face ugly and shapeless with fright, she knew that it was true.

Poor Sophie Lindgren was dead.

BOOK FIVE

One Time in Winter

15

Doctor Cadell was a very tall man. When he walked in the corridors, the evenly spaced lamps, bulbs behind curved moulds of dimpled glass, spread a uniform light; but once she had glimpsed him from a window walking on a bright cold morning, the moon like a white fingernail in the middle of an empty sky, going from this building to the administration block and his shadow which was hidden inside unrolled itself and leaping out stretched black upon the grass. The nurses used your first name; Sit up, How are we this morning? Drink it all, That's a good girl; but Dr Cadell, who would have more right than any of them, had never called her Lucy, not once. It was strange.

'Mrs Ure?' he said again.

'Thinking? Not about anything. I was wondering why you never call me by my first name.'

'Does that trouble you?'

'It doesn't matter.' There was a silence. 'Plenty of people call me by my first name, after all.' More silence. 'The nurses here. They use your first name. Without a by your leave.'

She thought he might pursue that. She knew sometimes she gave the impression of being arrogant, no, that was too flattering, she flattered herself, some people thought she was a snob.

'Do you think it special?'

What did he mean? 'Phatic communion,' she said. There was a silence. She was accustomed to these intervals, which would stretch until she filled them. She always did at last. Today she wondered what would happen if she kept silent. Not a word till the end of the hour.

'You would be making a mistake,' Dr Cadell said, 'assuming you ever want to go home.'

That she had spoken aloud frightened her. What he had said frightened her. It was a threat they might shut her up in a place like this for the rest of her life. But at once, with the thought came its rebuttal: I don't believe that. She had been unwell, but soon she would be going home. The thought popped into her head – perhaps he's irritated because he has never heard of phatic communion; they're often surprisingly ignorant these men. Not that he was, not that he was, not that he was; how angry he might be if he could look inside her head!

The truth was that he did frighten her.

'The anthropologist Malinowski,' she began. Behind the desk he had his back to the window and, although the daylight was feeble, the lamp angled towards her left his expression uncertain. 'People saying, Good morning to one another, or asking, How are you? It's not that they want to know. It's just a friendly noise. Saying someone's there.'

'Who do you think should be there?' Dr Cadell asked.

'Anybody.' She was puzzled, it was so obvious. 'Anybody except yourself.'

'Your husband, for example?'

'I wasn't talking about myself.'

'You feel we're here for some general philosophical discussion?'

'Anthropological,' she said, and for some reason finding that funny began to laugh and then could not stop and then was finished and listened again to the silence. 'I'm sorry,' she said.

'Do you know how long you've been here?'

'Just now?' She wasn't certain what he meant and, unsure, genuinely did not want to displease him. He did not answer, but made a sharp little jerk with his chin. It seemed to her a movement of irritation, even if he hadn't intended to show it. The boredom with her had just come out of him and that made it worse. 'In the hospital? You mean, in the hospital? If you mean in the hospital, I've been here for days, oh, days and days.'

'This is the seventh week.'

If he had thought to startle her, he had miscalculated. The days had a different texture from any before; the nights were outside time.

'Perhaps it's time to try something different,' he said.

They had kept her asleep at first. Later, they had given her a drug which made her hands spasm into claws. Lately, he had given her an hour of his time and at each session sat her in this low chair to look up at him against the light and talk about Maitland, her father, teachers she remembered from schooldays. She could not talk about things she did not remember. No one could expect her to do that.

'I don't want you to put electricity into my head,' she heard herself whisper.

'Nothing like that. We want you to remember, not forget.'

'"We"?'

'I want you to remember.'

She shook her head. 'I know who I am. I tell you about my childhood. About Maitland and me, how happy we are. There isn't anything wrong with me. I want to go home.'

'Your husband would want you to stay here until you are well.'

Dr Cadell made the point unemphatically, not giving it any importance, something as obvious as that. But the effect was disastrous.

'Maybe he has his reasons, reasons, called Janet, reasons called Janet!'

And she could have laughed and then she was appalled. It was an idea that had got into her head, a ridiculous idea; but things stayed in your head, like mice you didn't see them just a tremble of light to darkness in a corner and you knew one had found its way out of the field into the room with you; and ideas were like that, even ridiculous ones. And it should have been kept inside her head. And to make that noise, such a bitter sound. She had let herself down – and Maitland. Almost it would be better to be forgivably mad.

'Who is Janet?'

'Nobody, it doesn't matter.' But his silence told her it did. 'She's a neighbour. In the village where we live.'

'She's a young woman?'

'Not so young. Yes, younger than me. And pretty, before you ask. More than pretty. And no, I don't really think she's having an affair with my husband!'

'An affair. Was that what you meant when you talked about "reason"?'

'Isn't that what you thought I meant?' But he wasn't the one who was there to answer questions. 'If you want to know I feel sorry for her. We used to see one another quite regularly. She was my friend. Is my friend. Only she hadn't been – hadn't been out at all – round the village, I mean. There had been a party – and she was dancing – and then Ewen, that's her husband, he made a scene. Afterwards he hit her – when they were home that is, but people knew. He gave her a black eye. And then I was ashamed about not going to see her and I went and she was reading – I don't know how to describe it. Some silly story about pirates or highwaymen, but all just an excuse to write about sex. Do you know the kind of thing I mean? And poor Janet was sitting there in the middle of the morning, reading rubbish like that. Of course, I felt sorry for her.'

'She was pretty, you said.'

'. . . And younger than me,' said Lucy, who wasn't stupid and had been taught by implication the rules of this peculiar game.

'What conclusion do you draw from that?'

'I was jealous of her? . . . I never felt I was. Maybe when she talked about age, as if she was getting old. I would have swapped with her. I told her so, I'd cheerfully change

134

ages with you. But that's not anything. I think everyone feels like that. Men just as much as women.'

She had been staring down at her hands twisted together in her lap. Glancing up, she caught him making that same swift sideways jerk of the chin, by which perhaps he was only easing his neck, although it appeared to her still as a tic of boredom or exasperation.

'The night at the theatre,' he said, 'I am sure we are not going to progress until you can talk about what happened.'

'That thing about Janet,' she said, staving him off, 'I suppose it shows – it is hard to know—'

'Miss Lindgren was sitting beside you. She was among the volunteers who went up on to the stage for the performance. Shortly afterwards she died.'

'You told me I don't have much self-esteem. It seems it must be so. For whatever reason.'

'The first indication that something was wrong came from you. You began to scream.'

'I only know what you tell me.'

'You stood up and began to scream.'

'If I realised she was dead. There doesn't seem anything strange in that.'

'But you didn't stop. You were ill. You came here the next morning.'

She had learned from being with him that silence had a colour, pale and blue like ice. The silence in this room belonged to him and spread like ice, forcing you out of it.

'I don't remember.'

'With your consent, I should like to try another approach.'

And like a fool her first thought when he told her was, yes, there was a couch in the room. The first time she had come here she had noticed it against the wall. Expecting to be asked to lie down on it, she had been struck by how narrow it was, an uncomfortable-looking thing, lumpy in green leather.

'I don't think so,' she said. 'I wouldn't like that.'

'You prefer it as things are,' he said, not even making it

sound like a question, and spoke of her father and of Maitland; and it was true she had too little self-esteem to stand out against what he wished.

She did not have to stir out of the chair, only close her eyes at his suggestion. It seemed to take a long time, though, as he asked her to relax each limb in turn. '. . . You are going backward into the darkness,' he said, '. . . more and more comfortable, you are going backward and backward, backward and backward into the darkness and as you go backward you feel more and more comfortable, more relaxed, very relaxed, and hearing only my voice . . .'

She listened to him quite detachedly, not involved just listening, not with any sense of surrendering, nothing like that.

It seemed all she had to do was wait and it would come to her. In a moment, not to make her afraid but only so that she would understand. What had made her afraid enough to hide from it in madness.

And then a small quiet voice inside suggested perhaps after all there wasn't any need to go on. Really, there wasn't any need to go on, except that it was too late. She had wandered too near the edge . . . to where it was easy . . . and there was no way not . . . to slide over into the dark.

16

'Some people can't believe in the Resurrection. That's all right. There's no reason why you should. You're not even in the minority – not in this country now. Funny thing is, no one ever has any difficulty believing in the Crucifixion. Wouldn't it be nice if people refused to believe in the possibility of a man being crucified?'

The tiger pushing a face of eyes and teeth out between leaves the size of manhole covers had a purple flower tucked behind its ear. Lucy had been looking at it for a long time. All the prints around the walls were the same, writhing tangles of primary colours as if drawn by a child, but without innocence. Tiger, tiger, burning bright. A flame, pure, not muddled, not human. Then imitate the action of the tiger, men in night forests, men could turn themselves into something pure like a flame. Better to be a muddling human thing. Ash was dirty.

It was into that drift of half thoughts, sufficiently muddled, that the voice came and it surprised her that it should be speaking of resurrection in that place. The room was almost empty. It must be dry outside. People would be going back and forward on the paths. The woman who had spoken must be the one at the table by the door. She was in a dark skirt and blouse with a cardigan on top and was young. The man with her was in a dressing-gown and slippers, wrinkled pyjama legs between, one of them caught up to show a thick ankle white as suet.

The woman looked up and then away so quickly it seemed there must be a reason. She felt the woman had recognised her, and it was that rather than any recognition on her own side which fixed her gaze upon a pale heavy-featured face, a woman in her twenties, wearing unsuitable glasses.

While she was puzzling over it, the couple were getting up. The man's voice was soft and hasty with a tune to it that made it hard to follow. Thank you, he was saying, that was it, thank you and he was calling her doctor.

They were going.

'Please!' Lucy said.

The woman looked round at once, then said something to the man who left. It was as if she had been expecting Lucy to speak.

'I hate this room,' Lucy said. 'I'm sorry.'

'There's no need to be. I'm not responsible for it.'

'It's the smell of cigarettes.' Round the room on pedestals the ashtrays were layered with stale butts. 'It upsets my husband too, I know it does, though he doesn't say anything.'

The woman frowned, dark brows drawing together above the heavy frames of her glasses. 'Your husband isn't likely to be here now. Visiting hour is almost over.'

'Would you walk with me?' and as the woman hesitated Lucy heard herself pleading, 'I don't want to sit here on my own. And I haven't been outside for such a long time.'

'Perhaps not outside.'

Through the glass as they walked to the end of the first-floor corridor and back again, they could look down on patients and visitors circling the paths.

'Did you feel it wouldn't be appropriate? To be seen outside with me?'

This wasn't Lucy's floor, and she stared into a long ward as they passed. All the beds were empty except one which showed a bandaged head on the pillow. You couldn't tell if it belonged to a man or woman.

'It hasn't anything to do with "appropriate". If we walked out there, it might disturb some of my patients. You're not one of my patients.'

138

'I'm Dr Cadell's patient,' Lucy said.

'All the more reason.'

They came to the head of the stairs at the end of the corridor for the second time. Down below, the paths were emptying. Visiting time was over.

'Was he one of your patients?' Lucy asked. 'The man in the dressing-gown?'

'Yes, as a matter of fact.'

'Did you see him when you were passing the waiting-room?'

' "Happened to be passing", you mean. No, it wasn't by chance. He goes there every visiting hour, never misses – and no one has ever come to see him.'

'So you decided it was time someone did. That was kind of you.'

The woman plunged her fists into the pockets of the cardigan, looking offended. It was a vulnerable gesture, which had the odd effect of making her seem older than she had struck Lucy at first – in her thirties perhaps.

'Nothing to do with kindness. There were medical reasons.'

'You talked to him about religion. About the Crucifixion.'

'He's from Lewis,' the woman said, smiling as if that was enough of an explanation. The unexpected smile went away like a curtain being drawn as a group of nurses, chattering down from the upper landing, quietened to have a look as they passed. But for that moment, smiling, she seemed even younger than on the first impression, as if the sensible shoes, the heavy glasses and the cardigan were the props of a part she had been chosen to play.

One of the nurses said something and the high lightness of girls' laughter floated up to them. As if responding to the sound, the woman nodded in dismissal at Lucy and began to mount the stair.

'And walking with me,' Lucy said, though the woman went on without glancing back. 'I can't help thinking that was kind.'

If being in a room by herself was lonely, still Lucy felt it would have been worse to be in one of the public wards. When she got back, a nurse was there with a tray. 'You're late back,' she said. 'Time for your nap.'

Lucy unzipped her skirt and stepped out of it. Taking off her blouse she was embarrassed because the nurse was watching her; and that was a good sign, since it had not bothered her when she was ill. She put on the gown and bent to take off her pants, then sat on the edge of the bed and turned into it modestly. She had kept on her bra. Perhaps the nurse found her carefulness funny or was being irritated by her. There was no way of telling from the girl's round unsmiling face. All this time waiting without a word; perhaps she was paying no attention at all, her head full of thoughts of, no ring, some boy friend, old-fashioned word, live-in lover more like, or of a child, a ring meant nothing now, she might be a single parent. And all this time not speaking, just standing beside the bed, without a word. Lucy wondered if the fault was hers, if there was something in her which put people off so that they did not want to talk to her. Weren't nurses, after all, supposed to be great gossips? She did not even know the girl's name.

'Are you new?'

'New?' The nurse held out the little cup with the tablet in it, half red, half blue, like a bullet in party colours. 'That's right, right over, wash it down with a mouthful of this.'

'Perhaps you've been on one of the other floors?'

'No, I wouldn't say new. Do you want any more to drink?'

'I forget things. I've been sleeping so much.' The nurse was at the door ready to go. Lucy said, 'I have to be awake for the visiting hour.' Suddenly she was unsure of what day it was. 'There is a visiting hour this evening, isn't there?'

'Your husband here this afternoon?' Lucy nodded; it

140

was none of the girl's business. 'Twice in one day. He's faithful.'

'Oh, yes.'

When the girl had gone, it occurred to her that she might have been one of the nurses who had come chattering down the stairs earlier. She tried to bring back an image of them and at first couldn't fit the girl into it and then she was there. It kept changing back and forward; first the girl would be there and then not. She tried to keep thinking about it since she didn't want to fall asleep and miss Maitland in the evening. The woman doctor had been kind. She should have asked the nurse for the doctor's name.

Why? . . . Why was she so angry? Because she hadn't asked the nurse's name? It was herself she was angry with. Reluctantly, she came fully awake. No, it was the woman doctor's name. Not that it mattered. Still she had been kind and for no reason. Walking the corridor from one end to the other, the ward with the poor bandaged head on the pillow, alone while outside, the paths in the pale sunlight, busy with people.

She started up and without any willing or sense of transition was on her feet. It was dark outside and fat raindrops splashed in eye shapes on the glass. She had missed the visiting hour. Her legs began to tremble and, afraid of falling, she let herself down on to the edge of the bed. Slumped, she stared at the institutional darkness of carpet, tasting with a swollen tongue the sourness of drug sleep on her teeth.

A bustle of voices and the trolley's squeaking bore in on her slowly. She had just turned her head to listen when the door opened and they were there with the evening meal. 'This is hurry up night,' the girl said. 'Visitors'll be here soon.'

Later there was a row for not eating, only stirring the food on her plate. She had managed to force down no more than a mouthful or two.

'It's all I can manage. I would be sick.'

'That's just being silly.' The nurse, a different one from earlier, heavily built with wide hips and a roll of puppy fat under her chin, spoke as if to rebuke a child. 'Wasting good food. I've told you before.'

'I wasn't being silly,' Lucy said. Indignant, she made it sound as if she was quoting the girl and the last word came out as 'sully' in imitation of the broad local accent. Hearing it, she was ashamed of herself, would have liked to offer the girl an apology, only there were no easy words, for if it was an insult and felt as such by both of them yet what lay behind it was complicated not simple.

The nurse held out the tray, scowling down at the evidence of delinquency. 'You're supposed to eat.'

'Yes.'

'Right. If you didn't eat, you'd have to be made to eat.'

'But I do. It's just that I was sleeping. It's hard to have an appetite, sleeping so much. Usually I eat.'

The nurse let her finish. 'I didn't mean to frighten you,' she said. Lucy shook her head. The girl took the tray to the door and put it on the trolley. 'They put tubes into your nose,' she said. 'You'd think you wouldn't be able to breathe.'

Getting dressed was a slow business, but she was determined not to go to the visiting-room in a dressing-gown. She didn't want Maitland to see her like that any more. It was important he knew she was getting better. She rested for a moment before pulling on her skirt. It was true she had lost weight; the skirt hung slack on her hips. What the girl had said was nonsense, something she had gawped at on television. Suffragettes being force-fed. Nothing to do with what could happen to anyone in this brightly lit place. It was frightening, though. There was something there to be afraid of, for if someone in authority told her to do it, that girl would feed the tube down your throat and hold you down; do it cheerfully to someone who had mocked her accent. Not that anything like that could happen here, not here. An ignorant girl blethering

'I'm sorry,' she said.

In the silence, Maitland turned his face to her. What else could he be assuming but that she wanted forgiveness for the sick images of him and Janet together in bed, and the bed theirs, the bed in which he should struggle only with her? The regret she felt, in fact, was vaguer than that, and for something more encompassing.

It seemed to her that Maitland knowing her so well should feel how sorry she was for bringing them to this indignity.

The angle of the winter morning sun left one side of his face in shadow, distracting her. When she was shown in by the nurse, why had he given no sign of recognising how great was the shock of her surprise? Not to have been told he was going to be there was so unfair. If she had lost the right to the courtesy of being asked, then not even to be warned that he would be there. 'I felt it was better that your husband should be here this morning,' and Maitland not saying a word. The moment reran in her head, but this time Maitland held out his hands to her, kissed her on the cheek.

This time he stood up.

This time he stood up to welcome her.

To comfort her.

This time he stood up.

'There comes a time,' Dr Cadell was saying, 'when the barriers have to be broken down. Afterwards the healing, but first the breaking down. I explained to your husband why it would be helpful if he was present when I played the tape to you. He agreed.'

There was a tape recorder on the desk. She had not seen it before.

'This comes from our most recent sessions,' Dr Cadell said, 'when you were under hypnosis.'

'You didn't say anything to me about a tape.'

He shook his head at that, glancing towards Maitland. But you didn't! You didn't! She had to restrain herself from crying that out, in frustration like a child. You must have begun each time after I had gone to sleep; taking the machine from wherever it was concealed, perhaps from out of a drawer in the desk.

'Have you heard it already?' she asked Maitland.

Instead of answering he looked to Dr Cadell, who after the briefest of hesitations said, 'What you're going to hear is edited. It would take hours to play the full record, as many hours as the sessions lasted.'

It was obvious that he had already played the tape to Maitland. No doubt of that at all. She could understand the usefulness of being able to play back what had been said, could see it was no different in principle from taking notes on a case; but she felt it, in some kind, as a betrayal. If the act they were engaged in was whatever else also and as well only two people talking together, then what had been betrayed was trust. And why shouldn't there be a second recorder hidden and taping everything they said at this moment? Had Maitland thought of that?

Clever Maitland.

'I can see,' she said, 'that "the full record" of our sessions would be a bore. All those silences.'

There was a silence.

If she laughed they would be right to be angry with her. All the same laughter was there, like a tiny spool unwinding inside her, and that made it worse when Doctor Cadell pressed the switch and she began to understand what her voice was saying.

You watch then, that was what he said, and he took the nipple of her breast and hurt her. Yes, I felt the hurt though I wasn't supposed to, somewhere inside I felt it, somewhere inside. I've seen that before, one of the other men said. Open your eyes, Sleeping Beauty, he said to her.

'Why are you doing this?' she whispered. 'I won't listen to this.'

Good dog/can I touch her?/you're a lucky bitch/lift your leg – pee like the dogs do/finished with her? who's talking about finished with her? we haven't bleeding started on her it'll be a long time before we're finished with her a long time before I'm finished with her

156

And that ended it, all of it coming out in her own voice but flat and without emotion, as if looking down from above hearing those men and seeing what they did.

'Such vileness! It has nothing to do with us.' Ignoring her appeal, Maitland stared at the machine as if listening to the whine of its rewinding. Doctor Cadell pressed a button and the tape slid out into his hand. 'You have no right.'

And knew that he had.

'I want you to try to remember the night Sophie Lindgren died. Want you to try again,' he said.

'I've told you all I can.' This was familiar ground, an escape from the crippled fluttering effort to make sense out of the horror they had forced her to listen to. 'I hardly knew the girl.'

'So you tell me. So your wife has been telling me all these weeks,' he said to Maitland. 'Yet under hypnosis something very strange happens. "Lindgren", "Sophie", these words – it doesn't matter what the question is or the context I create – always produce the same response. What you just heard.'

On the edited tape, he had left only her voice; he was absent. 'You made me say these things,' Lucy whispered, and saw them exchange a glance.

'The girl in the room, the hypnotist, the other men, the indignities they subject her to – and every time the same scene, the same actors, playing out their parts without variation . . . every time it comes out in the same words, almost the same words.'

But when Lucy tried to see the face of the girl or the young man or the hypnotist she had nothing but her own voice metallic on a tape: not one of them had a face.

'Dreams have their own logic,' Dr Cadell was saying.

' "Dreams"?' Maitland harsh and sudden as in a seminar.

'Oh, don't think we haven't talked about them,' Lucy heard her voice shrilling. 'Not that my dreams were exciting. I think he found them dull.'

Dr Cadell studied her for a moment, then said to

Maitland, 'I mean by "dream" something that didn't happen.'

'None of that happened?'

Dr Cadell stared at him in surprise. 'Of course not.'

'I thought hypnotism was a way of getting at the truth.'

'A tool for finding it,' he leaned back in the chair, steepling his fingers, 'but there may still be some work to be done.' He's going to lecture Maitland! the thought struck Lucy as incongruous. Yet there the two men sat, holding one another's gaze – and not blinking, be sure of that. Really, she thought, for the moment at least I might as well not be here. 'The mind under hypnosis is still itself and full of complications. If he doesn't understand that, the hypnotist can lead the patient without intending to do so and be told what he wants to hear. The police, before they knew what they were doing, got themselves into trouble with that. They imagined at first hypnotism was going to be an infallible lie detector to sniff out the truth for them.'

'You're not suggesting my wife felt that obscene story would please you?'

'Hardly . . . No, I'm suggesting the mind defends itself from things it can't bear to deal with.' And suddenly she wasn't a spectator any longer for he looked at her and her safety was over. He held up the tape. 'I'm suggesting there was something about Sophie Lindgren's death that your wife couldn't face.'

That awful sigh, it had driven her mad. But just at that moment, about to tell them of it, Lucy knew what was wrong. The two men were speaking as if this was the first time they had listened to the tape together. That was false.

'My wife has told you she hardly knew the girl.'

'But she knew of your relationship with Miss Lindgren.'

Maitland shook his head. 'No.'

They watched her, the two men. Speaking the words they had rehearsed, they watched her.

'But there was a relationship.'

'My wife knew nothing of it.'

'I think she must have.'

How did they want her to react? The significance of what they were saying was muffled for her. Was she to be shocked? Words in a play acted for her benefit. For her benefit, surely in every sense. Whatever the words meant, the intention was to help her to be well.

It would have been easier if she had been unaware of what they were doing. Then it would have been easier for Dr Cadell to help her.

She was more intelligent than he realised, than they realised.

'Isn't that so?' She realised he had been waiting for her to respond.

'I thought we were happy together,' she said, not looking at Maitland.

'It's possible to know and be determined not to know.' He had steepled his fingers again. It was her turn for a lecture. 'It would explain why you found her death so traumatic. You wanted it to happen – when it did, you went into shock.'

'Is it true then?' she asked Maitland.

'More than that,' he said. 'It's general knowledge. Sam Wilson was obliging enough to help the police with their enquiries by telling them about Sophie and me. I'm sorry.'

Sam Wilson, so busy in the Department, but not distinguished, he hadn't published anything worth reading, so Maitland said, and he ran around after Maitland, made such a fuss of admiring him—

'How could he be so disloyal!' she cried.

Instead of Maitland, she was accusing Wilson (and it was true; the little wretched creature). It didn't mean she had missed the enormity of what Maitland had admitted. The thing about Wilson just something she had blurted out. But even so. And Maitland hadn't smiled. If she had been Maitland, listening she might have smiled. No wonder if even the best of men despised women a little.

'Mrs Ure?' She was listening, yes, she was listening. 'It was after our sessions of hypnosis that I made it my business to find out the details of the Great Sovek's performance that

159

evening. I made a prediction to myself that there would be someone persuaded to impersonate a dog. I thought it might have been a woman. In fact, it was a young man. When Sophie Lindgren died, he was on all fours – just as you describe your girl in the "dream" to be – on all fours beside her. She died with him beside her like that.'

She saw him. On all fours. His head nuzzled between the girl's legs.

'Are you all right?' It was Maitland's voice, very far away.

'Was it you who killed her?' she asked him.

'She killed herself!' It was exactly the note with which he would respond when he found something she had said exasperatingly ridiculous.

'It was you who saw that something was wrong,' Dr Cadell said. 'No one else was watching her with such a . . . *jealous* attention. You knew she was your husband's mistress.' He glanced at Maitland. 'We really must accept that somehow you had learned about it. To see her die like that when you were so full of anger against her. It must have been traumatic. Anger and the desire to punish, they're still there in the treatment of the girl in the "dream". In throwing it up as a defence it also allows you to work out your aggression against me. I am the hypnotist prying into secrets – so you turn me into a monster. It explains everything.'

But Lucy was not listening. Instead she watched his smile that had slipped out, secretive, satisfied, despite himself.

No one tells me the truth, she thought. What if there has been a trial and I've been found guilty? Guilty but insane. A husband takes a young woman to love; why wouldn't men believe I killed her? The poor wife. Poor madwoman.

What if the hospital I remember out there isn't the real one? What if every door is locked behind me, every window barred?

Guilty but insane.

Inside she began to scream.

20

'What did he say then?' Anne Macleod asked.

'That it could only be what he called a dream. Not something that could ever have happened.'

But there were no images of a girl on all fours crouched naked as there would have been in a dream; just words, her own voice in her head, like a child reciting the stages of a Black Mass by rote.

'Why not?'

Lucy hadn't expected that question, the tone of cool enquiry, the sharp glance that went with it.

'Because it was sick. Horrible.'

'That's what he said?' And when Lucy shook her head. 'No, he knows sick things happen inside heads and outside them. Inside first and after a time someone goes and does them. Outside and they get to be part of dreams, even the ones you don't know you have.'

'He told me no one can hypnotise you and make you do something that was wrong. You would wake up. Doctor Cadell told me that. If you were asked to do something wrong.'

'I read about an experiment once—' Anne Macleod paused as a nurse clattering out from one of the side wards looked at them curiously. They were in the upper corridor again, walking it from one end to the other as they had done before. 'It was at one of those American universities with an exotic name – Tulsa, I think. The experimenter had a beaker of sulphuric acid. He told each subject what it was. Just to make sure there could be no doubt, he put a strip of zinc into the acid.' And Lucy was able to picture that: white fumes steaming out like a mad horror film. 'He told them, this would scar, it could burn the eyes out of your head. Then he hypnotised them and told them to throw the beaker in his face. And some of them did.'

'How could they?' Lucy protested.

'After they were hypnotised, a glass screen was slid up between him and each of them. The subjects didn't know anything about it. There was one man who threw with such force the acid splashed all across the glass.'

'I don't believe—' Lucy began. 'Your experimenter couldn't be sure – how could he be sure? I'm sure the man who threw the acid knew the screen was there.'

Anne Macleod made no answer to that, and coming to the last window in the corridor they looked down to where a man with a stick was spearing up rubbish from the lawns.

'If it had been me – anyway, if it had been me,' Lucy said, 'I couldn't have thrown – even if I'd realised the glass was there. Not acid. The idea is too horrible. Of hurting someone in that way.'

'That man who threw the acid. He was a big man – one of those football players who get scholarships to American universities. And then he finds he has to do this as part of the course. And he is one of those who go under and can't seem to resist. I imagine he might be angry without knowing it. Being hypnotised perhaps just gave him permission to do what he really wanted to do – punish the lecturer who was doing these things.' The man below gathered up the mouth of a sack and began to drag it behind him across the winter pale grass. 'It isn't everyone who can be hypnotised really deeply. To walk around and do things, and then remember none of it once you're out of the trance. Sleepwalkers and amnesiacs. Somnambules they're called. They're quite rare. I imagine Sophie Lindgren might have been one,' Anne Macleod said.

Lucy turned away from her, going back the way they had come, hurrying. 'Do you think,' she wondered aloud, hearing the footsteps behind her, 'she was sleepwalking when she went to bed with my husband?'

She felt herself caught by the sleeve. She stopped unresisting in front of a ragged poster taped on to a pinboard beside a yellowing page of fire regulations.

'Lucy?'

'I don't need you to tell me I'm mad as well. You're not my doctor.'

'If you shook any of Cadell's patients,' Anne Macleod said, and did take Lucy by the arm and shake her, 'you'd hear the pills rattle about inside them. Pimozide. Chlorpromazine. Thioridazine. Trifluoperazine. Haloperidol. Fluphenazine. Sulpiride.'

'And yours, are yours different, aren't your patients just the same?'

'All the same,' Anne Macleod frowned, nodded her head fiercely. 'I work here. I'm not in charge. A hundred years ago in places like this doctors cut out the womb as a cure for hysteria. No women doctors then.' She thrust her fists into the pockets of her coat. 'Not that things change much. Most of the patients are still women. Most of the doctors men.'

But before Lucy could absorb that, in the way of quiet corridors there was a sudden flurry of activity. An orderly came whistling from the lifts shoving an empty wheelchair along one-handed; while from the other direction three women in dressing-gown and slippers shuffled softly nearer. The one in the middle looked familiar, someone from the lower corridor, shuffling forward like an inquisitor – what are you doing here? what are you talking about?

Before they came level, Anne Macleod walked away, lingering just for an instant to be seen taking a look, a last look as if checking something, at the poster, the torn poster, its needle and skulls.

Later, alone in her room, Lucy lay on the bed listening to the sounds in the corridor.

Acid can burn the eyes out of your head.

And then she had said, Being hypnotised gave him permission.

163

21

It was Anne, Doctor Macleod, who had told her.

'There was no need for us to have to meet in the visitors' room. You could have come here, all the time you could have come here. This is a private room. Didn't you know that?'

'Since I'm paying for it,' Maitland said.

'I'm sorry.'

'What about?'

'For all of this.' The tears came and she knew how he hated that; but they wouldn't stop. She pressed her hands against her cheeks under her eyes. She felt the tears slide down between her fingers as if to open them.

'You'll be coming home soon.' The words were said to comfort her and that must be kind. What she needed though was for him to touch her. Not even leaning forward he sat in the chair facing hers between the bed and the window. Something in the arrangement of it, the chairs too near the bed, made her think of a room in a cheap hotel; some cramped place where lovers lay waiting for morning.

'I don't know what's wrong with me,' she wept.

'You had no idea about Sophie and me?'

'If I had known, I would have wanted her dead.' The back of her throat spasmed and she could have vomited, lowering her face to hide that from him. 'Isn't that Doctor Cadell's theory?'

They sat in silence.

'Only you didn't know.'

'I went mad for some other reason.'

'Don't talk like that,' he said. It wasn't an appeal, but a reproach; or his habit of telling her what should be done. She had not yet shaken off the habit of responding. For the long-married, habits it seemed were what survived.

'I told Doctor Cadell about the time Daddy sent me to fetch his briefcase, when he set up the mask to frighten me.'

'What?' Blank. Frowning.

'I told you about it.' A long time ago; when lovers laid claims upon one another by the things they confided.

'But you were just a child.'

'Why not? That's the time they're keen on hearing about.'

'"They".'

'People like Cadell. For them that's the important time. Far more than what happens to you later. Like adultery.'

Maitland stood up abruptly.

'It's not fair of you to be angry with me in this place. There was this woman at the dispensary this morning. When should I take my tablets? she asked. The pharmacist told her, Take them at eight and six. Oh, no, she said, my people tell me to take them at lunchtime. And she was crying and started to shout. I was standing beside her.'

The door opened and the nurse appeared, her heavy features lightening into a simper at sight of Maitland. 'Doctor Cadell would like to see you for a moment. Your wife won't be alone. Another visitor's come.'

He was gone before she could say a word. By turning her head, only a little movement, she could see through the window a patch of lawn sloping up into a bank of uncut grass and then the drab wall of a long single-storey ward. Once she had been sitting on the edge of the bed and looked up to see a man at the window opposite. She had been in her nightdress, but he wouldn't have seen her; it was hard to see into a room. Waiting, she tried not to think of how she would cope when the nurse brought Janet. She knew it must be Janet and that she would say,

Why do you keep hanging on to him? You know he doesn't want you any more.

When Monty Norman came in, her first reaction was relief.

'Gone to see the doctor, has he? I'll sit with you for a bit. All this long time, they haven't been allowing you visitors. You could say this was my first chance.' He bent over and she felt his hand cool on her forehead, his breath on her cheek. 'You can sleep if you want to.'

22

The sigh was her own sigh coming with the last breath of her life passing out of her mouth into the stale crowded air.

Dying came harder. When she opened her eyes there was the white length of her arm and the tube rising from it to the bag of the drip. It looked so strange she reached to touch it, and a hand caught hers and put it firmly under the blanket.

'Be a good girl,' the nurse said.

Next time she came awake, a woman stood over her making a clenched fist from which there stuck out the glittering point of a needle. 'Don't hurt me,' she said, before recognising who it was.

The drip went into a junction valve set into her arm and by lifting her head she could see where the tube entered and that there was a second opening into which Anne Macleod was sliding a syringe.

'Vitamin B 12,' she said. 'We have to make sure you haven't damaged your liver.'

Lucy tried to sit up and groaned at a spasm of pain.

'Tummy sore? You had to be pumped out.'

'What is the drip for?'

It seemed important to know, not to slip under without finding out why they had done this to her.

'You'll be on that for twenty hours. It's an antidote.'

'Why?'

'Against the stuff you took.'

'Like poor Sophie.'

'Not quite,' Anne Macleod said, 'but very nearly.'

23

She dreamt that she was on a stage with a man on his knees in front of her lapping like a dog between her legs. A hand brushed the hair back from her face, stroked her forehead, the tips of fingers traced the line of her cheek. She jerked away and opened her eyes. Anne Macleod on the chair beside the bed straightened and sat back from her.

'How are you feeling?'

'I didn't know she killed herself like that.'

'With tablets. Stolen from in here. Like you. Not the same kind, though.' They were talking about Sophie Lindgren, of course; and Lucy took it for granted that had been understood, as if she had resumed a conversation they had already begun. 'Otherwise you would be dead.'

'I'm grateful to be alive. I'll never do that again.'

'I've heard people say that before.'

'Believe me.'

'That's not what I meant. Someone is found in a coma, brought into a hospital. They get pumped out, all the things that should be done, I did so much of that when I was in emergency, but we know it's too late. And when they come round they say, Thank God, I'm alive, I'll never do that again. And you look at them and you know they won't, they won't get any chance, they're already dead. Within days they're brought in again. The liver's gone.'

'Is that me?' Terror of dying stilled her.

'It might have been.' Anne Macleod sat silent and then her mouth opened in a movement like a yawn, and she sighed, a long trembling like the beginning of a sob. As Lucy stared up at her, she looked aside and her voice when she started to speak was harsh. 'Or brain damage. You were risking more than dying.'

'But I'm going to be all right.' Let doctors be contemptuous or angry with her: one of the self-wounded when so many others were injured and ill. What did it matter? Let them feel what they liked. Her life had been given back to her.

She hardly listened as Anne Macleod talked about how negligent the hospital had been in its overseeing of drugs. Bad record keeping, unlocked cabinets, an atmosphere so casual that Sophie had been able to steal the drugs which killed her.

'It wasn't the publicity Cadell had been hoping for, but things had been getting worse for ages. The truth is it was a scandal waiting to happen. And now you,' Anne Macleod said. 'After all the changes, it wasn't supposed to happen again.'

'Why was she here? Was she ill?'

'All of you were here. Don't you remember? Your husband, the man Norman, the little secretary woman, and the others with the Trust, you all turned up to collect the patients for the theatre visit.'

'I don't remember.'

'There were drinks, you were here for almost an hour. Doctor Cadell made an occasion of it.'

As if there was something to be defended, Lucy said, 'The Trust has had connections with the hospital since Charles Gregory's time.'

'They think she swallowed the tablets when we were with the Great Sovek or maybe in the bar at the interval. But the tablets came from here, there wasn't any doubt of that. There were articles in the papers. Visits from the Health Board.'

'Sophie Lindgren killed herself.' She wasn't real to Lucy any more; she couldn't even remember her face.

'After she died,' Anne Macleod said, 'I couldn't stop

169

thinking about her. I had seen a pretty girl, that was all I had seen, I hadn't seen any of her unhappiness, and I had been trained to see. It was such a waste. Maybe I could have done something, I couldn't stop thinking that.'

What was real was that she had been a girl, only a girl, with all of her life before her.

'Poor girl,' Lucy said.

What is real, Lucy Inside said, is that I'm alive.

24

When he came in she was afraid, but he sat down with his hands on his knees and looked across the bed at her. She had been waiting in the chair by the window, and at sight of him she started up then sank back not sure of what he might do if she tried to leave. Keep calm, she told herself, someone will come.

'I'm in a room with three other people. You have this to yourself, all right for some.'

The lights were on in the ward opposite, but there was no one to be seen, no one ever showed at any of the windows. A drizzling rain wept down on the grassy bank. Her glance snatched backed to him; he hadn't stirred. In this place full of people, she thought, I could be raped. The corridor outside was busy; nurses tapheeling past and no one to know what was being done in here. Drymouthed, she contemplated the idea of screaming.

'Not much of a view,' he said, getting up and coming to the window. She tried not to flinch, feeling the heat of his body standing close beside her. 'Better view from the roof when we were up there together.' And casually, in the same tone, 'You frighten easily. One kiss, I didn't mean to frighten you.'

'I'm waiting for my husband to come,' Lucy said. 'He's late. He should be here by now.'

'Funny time for a visit,' the Lewisman said, and ran his hand over the stiff brush of his hair while squinting at her sceptically.

'He's coming to take me home.'

'Cured, are you?' With a grin, he shook his head, did not believe that for a moment.

'I'm going home.'

'You're not committed. No reason why you shouldn't walk out the door. If your husband wants you back? If he's feeling lonely?'

'He's coming to take me home.'

'Well, then,' he said, a comfortable there-you-are-then noise that conveyed his doubt. 'And the children?' She said nothing, sure he was mocking her. 'You'll be looking forward to seeing them, their arms round you, putting their arms round you, hello, Mum!'

'Yes,' she said, and saw him frown. 'My two children. My daughter and my little boy.' She held out her hands and they were on either side of her, felt little hands, baby hands, and looked down and saw hers were empty.

And all the time he was talking.

'When I was in London, I went to this house one morning and knocked on the door. It was a terrace kind of a thing. I went there on the train, took me an hour and then there was a walk. I knew where I was going, though, they'd given me a bit of paper with it all written out – turn right out of the station, four streets along and then go left up the hill. There were black guys all over the place, coming back with the papers or out in the street washing the car. It was the middle of a Sunday morning. I thought just my luck if he's not in. Anyway, I came to the house, checked the number. It was red brick, you know the way, with a kind of cellar below and I went up the steps and rang the bell. The funny thing is when he opened the door he knew right away who I was though we'd never seen one another before. He went the colour of that sheet. "Tell Bernie I'll get the money," he said, "first thing in the morning." I showed him the shooter. "It has to be now," I told him. "For Christ's sake," he said, "not in front of the kids." And right enough a boy and girl had come up the stair into the hall – from the kitchen, I suppose. The girl had a cup in her hand. The boy might have been three or four, I'm no judge. In his underpants, nothing else on, standing there taking it all in. "You wouldn't shoot me in front of the boy?" that's what he said, "You wouldn't shoot me in front of the boy?" ' The Lewisman made a face of disgust. 'And he started crying. What do you make of that?'

'Did you kill them?'

She was so intent upon his answer she didn't realise someone had come into the room until he backed off, stepping right away from her.

'What are you doing here?' When she was excited, Anne Macleod's voice sounded more Highland, lengthening some of the vowels into a lilt.

'I came in to say, Look after yourself, all the best. She's going home today. Isn't that right? That's what she told me.'

'It doesn't matter what she told you.'

Lucy thought, they sound like brother and sister, though she knew another listener might hear the difference between them, coming from islands parted by miles of Atlantic sea set differently to the sun.

The Lewisman nodded. Shrugging and grinning like a caught schoolboy, he was making ready to leave.

But Lucy had to know. 'Did you?' she asked again. 'Did you kill them?'

He had to bend his head down to catch what she was saying. 'Didn't kill anybody. He paid up. He knew I would have done it, you see.' Then, as if, that out of the way, he had time to remark on what she had said, 'What do you mean "them"? I wouldn't ever hurt a child. Don't you know what Jesus said? "Better a millstone round your neck and be thrown into the sea." ' He straightened up and spoke to Anne Macleod. 'I'd throw them in with my own hands.'

'You shouldn't be here,' Lucy told him. That this hypocrite should hector them about Jesus gave her a moment of disgust which stood her in stead for courage. 'You have no right.'

173

'I tell you, doctor, this one has some funny visitors.' He clucked his tongue in disapproval. 'It was that set me thinking about London. I met a lot of people when I was in London.'

Lucy tried to meet his look, but its blank intensity defeated her.

'Please,' she said to Anne Macleod.

'How did it feel?'

'What?' What was he asking her?

'Stop this, Fraser,' Anne Macleod said. 'Your hear me?'

'I don't care why you did it. You did it with tablets, isn't that right? I was just wondering how it felt. What were you thinking about when you took them?'

Wearied by fright, she stumbled upon the simple truth. 'I watched my hands moving. It didn't matter what I was thinking.'

He turned that idea over, rubbing his hand back and forward over his scalp, staring down at her. In the end, nodded; one sharp jerk of the head. 'I can understand that.'

Explain it to me then. Make me understand.

But before she could say anything, Maitland was there at last. In jagged strokes rain rattled the window glass and smoked over the banks of lawn. The Lewisman looked out at it, hands at ease clasped behind him, his back turned to the room. *Pretending*: the word hissed viciously in Lucy's head.

'Oh, Maitland,' she said, 'take me home.'

'What's going on?' Maitland asked Anne Macleod.

'This is a sad lady,' the Lewisman said, turning from the window. She felt the weight of his hand upon her shoulder. 'I hope you look after her with kindness.'

'Do you, indeed?' When Maitland came across the room, he was by a full head the taller man. 'Obviously, you're not a doctor. A patient?'

'I'm not ashamed of that.' But it sounded like bluster.

The hand was still resting on her shoulder, and Maitland

174

reached out and lifted it away. Over his shoulder he said to Anne Macleod, 'My God, a patient.'

'Fraser Allander,' the Lewisman said, and went on like a threat, 'Your wife and I've become friends.'

'I really don't have time for this.'

'I wouldn't want her mixed up with the wrong people. I was saying to the doctor your wife has some funny visitors.'

Maitland beckoned to Anne Macleod. 'Time to take this one back wherever he came from. Now would be best.'

Still not having found a word to say, she came forward, a dull red patch high on each cheek. And the Lewisman went with her. Went so quietly it would have been easier to believe it was only fantasy, all his talk of guns and London.

25

On the eighth day after coming home, Lucy walked down through the woods behind the house and came upon three weasels strung up on a stock fence. They looked fresh, only one had the eyes pecked out, the red fur still sleek along each slim length. With a hook of barbed wire stuck in under the chin, they hung with their backs to the open view of green gently rolling fields and the hills further off. Lucy held out a finger to touch one, then drew it back; even dead, the narrow mouth ragged with needle teeth looked ready to scream and tear.

A stick snapped on the slope behind her. Under the footstep of an animal, she thought, a heavy animal; Janet coming down in search of her. If she kept still – crouched down like a bird on the open moor, so still you could pass close by and not see.

'Lucy?'

The voice came softly, uncertainly. She recognised it at once, though it was almost the last one in the world she might have expected.

'It is you,' Anne Macleod said, peering forward as if short-sightedly, her body braced against the run of the slope. 'I might have gone past and never known you were there.'

'Have you heard?' Lucy asked, and saw at once that she had not.

Anne came down the last of the slope to stand on the dry-stone dyke that acted as a retaining wall holding back the earth of the hill. She looked down at Lucy standing in the gap between the dyke and the fence.

'I went to your house,' she said, 'and knocked but no one was in.'

'No.'

'Could we sit here?' On the wall she meant. 'I have such a lot to tell you.'

For answer, Lucy hooked one heel on a jutting stone and hitched herself up, then shuffled along on her bottom until she settled on one flat and wide enough to be comfortable.

Anne swung down beside her, then said, 'Oh, God. God, how disgusting.'

Lucy looked at her in fright and then realised she was staring at the weasels strung on the fence.

'The keeper on the estate does it,' she said. Moles were hung too with their soft little paws held up by their chest. And different kinds of birds. Once she had seen a gull with the hook of wire thrust in under its beak. After a time one of its wings came off and lay on the ground under the fence.

'There's no need for it,' Anne said.

'If you heard a rabbit scream at night?'

'They don't do it for the rabbits.'

'No.'

That was true.

In the parkland beyond the fence a peacock came pacing between the trees. Lucy looked again and it wasn't there. Imagination. Not entirely, though, for on occasion they wandered from the drives around the estate house beyond the line of trees. Last year, sitting in almost this spot, she had watched one out there all alone, canopy of feathers glittering and vibrating in the senseless fury of its passion as it turned and turned in search of a rival.

'I've been to London,' Anne said.

It wasn't cold, a watered sunlight spread on the grass; but this early in the year the air was raw. Lucy shivered and clutched shut the collar of her coat. Instantly she felt

Anne's arm go across her back, hold her by the shoulder and draw her close.

Even by Maitland she disliked being touched, not in lovemaking, not in lovemaking, but like this casually, touches and embraces. She winced from them, fur rubbed the wrong way. Like a cat, he said.

'After your husband had taken you away – taken you home,' Lucy struggled to follow the sense of the words coming so softly they were almost whispered, 'Fraser Allander told me he had recognised one of your visitors. That's Mr Norman, I said. No, no, it isn't, Fraser said. I kept thinking about what he told me. He enjoyed telling me. I thought about nothing else and then I had three days off together and that's when I went to London.' And at last she lifted her arm away. 'It's cold, too cold here. Aren't you cold?'

Freed, Lucy tried to stop her teeth from chattering as she spoke, her body still clenched tight on itself. 'If you have something to tell me, come to the house.'

'Your husband won't be there?. . . Lucy?'

Wind stroked the fur of the hung weasels.

'No.'

'If he's there, we'll have to go somewhere else. Some of it's about him, Lucy.'

'No, he won't be there.'

Wondering when, or if she would tell her at all that Maitland must already be dead, Lucy watched the staring peacock turn and turn in the empty field.

BOOK SIX

Anne Macleod's Story

26

One of her patients had conceived the idea that torture, rape and unkindness (his own word, however much of an anticlimax in that list) were caused by pornography leaking from his mind and contaminating the whole world. A timorous man, in his mid-forties, his marriage childless, the worst of his sins was to work his way through the personal service numbers in *Forum*. 'There was this young man offering massage. A London number. It was early in the morning – my wife was still in bed, I closed the door so she wouldn't hear. When he answered, I asked him how much, things like that and then I asked, "I like to be knocked about a bit, is that all right?" And he said, yes. I was *corrupting* him, you see.'

A change from the ones who heard voices.

Not that he was mad, of course.

Nothing like it. And given permission by the situation, the hospital, the room, her job, to unload all of that sad triviality on to her. Like priests who were perhaps helped by having a tariff to charge against what they heard, celibate men listening and afterwards in the street able to match faces to whispers out of the warm dark; each one no more than a boy himself on that side of the partition for the first time with a tariff and a headful of transgressions in Latin to guide him, a driving instructor who wasn't supposed ever to get into the car. Or like ministers who divided in her memory into the ones who because they weren't compelled to listen found endless excuses not to and the ones, the one, say John Gardiner, who did.

Who had done. Those ones, that one, without a driver's manual in Latin or a tariff to apply must find it hard. He had found it hard. Thinking about him she understood as she had not understood when she was sixteen how hard it must have been to be a minister on that island, the inheritor of Calvinist certainties, another manual. So much for stereotypes: a Free Church minister on that island who found as a law of his nature the necessity for compassion. Compassion for all the weaknesses of creaturely flesh. Yet still had his map marked sin, guilt and redemption. It was not John Gardiner's fault that compassion was not enough. She had set out to find her own map.

'Rogerian therapy. Trained in New York,' the man astonishingly said. Earlier he had challenged her to guess what he did. 'Give you a clue,' he offered, inviting her to observe as he unscrewed the miniature of gin one-handed before emptying it into the plastic beaker. Beyond him she could look down on an enormous unmade bed of clouds rumpled white under the sun.

'Are you a barman?' she asked. She had intended to be rude, but he nodded and smiled at her quickness. Vaguely ashamed, she let herself be harassed into admitting in her turn that she was a psychiatrist.

A dentist had confessed to her once – at his place not hers; no couches; her lying back, mouth full of wadding and clamps of steel – that he was tired of doing his job, a young man's game, later you felt the tension even too much the fear of the patients: It affects you; We have a high incidence of stress-related illnesses in the profession. Too many mouths with evil breath? But he hadn't said that, had he? Going too far that would have been. Considering he was bent over with his nose almost in her mouth. Later came the sting on her lip where he had torn it with the clamp while it was anaesthetised. As if dentists were the only ones to wonder if they might have chosen the wrong profession.

'I am,' the man said, 'but I did the training. When I was in New York. You might sit for an hour and say nothing.

Not a word – and that would be *all right*. At the end pack up and go off and the psychiatrist will think, that was a good session. You have to be getting close to someone to be able to sit for an hour and say nothing. In a bar, though, people talk. Customers say things to me they wouldn't tell their wives.'

Too much evil breath coming out of mouths at you. In the old days students at Glasgow University who had come to the city from the islands would very often become tubercular, coughing up their lungs in cold digs. They lacked the immunity of those who had grown up in the place. They had no protection against sickening.

At Heathrow she let herself be carried along. The overnight bag was light enough to have let her stride as on previous visits feeling the brisk edge of speed until the moving track discarded her with a bump. This time she stood head bowed and let herself be carried along: to the end of the track, to the train, into an hotel. Bent over the washbasin gasping she threw up cupped handfuls of water until, lifting her head, eyes in the mirror surprised her with their blank suddenness of enquiry.

And after all, when she ventured out it was already getting dark and it might have been better to wait until the next day. *A to Z of London* in one hand, finger keeping the page, she climbed the stairs from the Tube and went back along Chalk Farm Road in the direction of Camden until she recognised the name of a street.

The first marker she came to was the church he had told her about: set back from the road, with a flattened spire, crouching behind a moat of scant grass. And the pub was where he had said it would be and she turned left and found the shop. The glass was dirty and the window empty apart from a Coke can squeezed and lying on its side. She couldn't see into the shop for a curtain pulled all the way along the back. Light leaked around the ragged edge of it. The door had boards nailed over, but when she gave a push it opened. The light went out.

'You on your own?' A-ow-wn: drawn out in a Bow Bells tune.

'Yes.' She stared into the dark. Listening she heard breath snort and whistle; adenoids, she decided automatically.

'What d'you want?' The voice sounded young.

'I'm a friend of Fraser Allander's.'

'Who?' But before she could answer, 'You mean Jock the Hat?'

It seemed likely. 'I expect so.'

Light dazzled her. Like a stretched string whoever was behind it walked the line to her. 'Come inside if you're coming.' She moved forward and the door was shut behind her. A key turned in the lock. The torch went out and there was darkness again and a spinning catherine wheel of colours, and then the overhead light was switched on.

To her surprise she had to look up at him. He was young but tall and thin. The most striking thing about his pale narrow face was the boil that inflamed the wing of one nostril, an aching red with a vesuvius of yellow pus in the centre. Visibly it seemed to throb. 'You talk funny the way he did. Sure you're his friend? Sure you're not his missus, something like that?' the boy said all on one breath. Boy? He might easily be in his middle twenties, perhaps even older, but he looked seventeen.

'Nothing like that,' she said. The shop was stripped, nothing on the counter, nothing on the shelves, nothing to steal. 'I thought this was where you held your meetings.'

'Who?'

'The Party.'

'Who?'

'Pax Britannica.' Absurd name. 'Fraser told me it met here.'

'And if it did?'

'I was interested in what he told me. I wanted to find out more.'

'Not because you heard Kite speaking?'

184

'No.'

'You surprise me. Got a treat in store, you have.'

He jerked his chin and she obeyed the invitation, following him across to the bead curtain that shut off the back shop. It clattered apart and together for him and then she was through. A little square room with a table and eight or nine chairs scattered about.

'It's not a Party,' the boy said, standing by the light switch.

There was a sink and a kettle with the flex wound round it, some cups, and a jar of instant coffee.

'More like a Movement. That's what Kite says.'

'Does he?' she speculated; but he seemed vigorously serious, the livid nostril going up and down like a signal lamp with the nodding of his head.

'You won't find anybody here tonight though. Lucky to find me. I'm just checking up on the premises.'

'I thought this was the night you met. That's what Fraser told me.'

The boy's head changed direction, shaking now from side to side. With a nose like that, the thought occurred to her, you'd think he'd find it painful.

'Not tonight. There's something on.' He furrowed his brow. 'You could come. Don't see why not.'

'You're meeting somewhere else?'

'Something like that.' He reached back through the curtain and the light in the shop went out. Before she realised what he was about to do, he struck down the switch beside him as well. Next moment the torch went on again.

'Right. Follow me. We have to go out the back way.'

'What?'

She stumbled and felt him touch her arm.

'Steady the buffs.' The light shone on a lock and then he had opened the door and they were outside. They began to pick their way along a lane, walls close on either side. Fear stirred, not for anything this ungainly boy might do

185

but that he would be no protection against the dangers of the dark.

It was a relief to emerge into a lit street.

'Steady the buffs?' she asked abruptly. 'Wherever did you get that from? Your father?'

'Leave it out.' He walked away from her, and when she caught him up repeated, 'You can leave that right out.'

Glancing up at him, she thought, of course, stupid of me. To an experienced eye he had the gangrel look of someone lacking a father or, more likely, with one it would have been better not to have known.

After a block walked in silence, she ventured, 'Why did we have to come out that way? Wouldn't it have been easier to leave by the front door?'

She had almost given up, when the mutter came from above her head. 'Had to. Essohpee.'

'I'm sorry, I don't understand.'

'Standard Operating Procedure. Essohpee. All right?'

And from the tone she understood that he was mollified.

Hurrying after him as he veered across the road to a parked van, she wondered if he was about to steal it. He seemed the type, and too feckless not to be caught if he tried. It was good to see the battered wing and the parking with two wheels canted on to the pavement. To confirm it was his, he produced keys and slid open the driver's door.

'Could you climb in this way? The other door's jammed,' he said.

He told her his name was Nick and asked hers. She laid her bag on the bench seat between them and then lifted it and laid it in her lap. It began to drizzle and between the lagging smear of the wipers shopfronts slid by and light gleamed from the slick of a deserted crossroads. After that there was a long empty street and then another of low brick houses and curtained windows.

'Is it far?' She heard her voice thin and rise; and steadying it asked, 'To the meeting?' He changed gears, turning into another dim street under the rain, no different from the one they had left. 'It is open to the public? I mean I took that for granted. In a hall or something.'

The van, however, instead of picking up speed was slowing and now came to a stop. Nick bent across her to peer out of the side window. There was a forecourt with petrol pumps, a workshop to one side and a place to pay on the other: all of it unlit.

'Bound to be out in a minute,' Nick said to himself. He leaned back. 'Wouldn't thank me for going in, I don't expect.' He extended a thin wrist and angled his watch to catch the light. 'Spot-on when he told me.'

Time passed while he sighed and fidgeted, but it was she who saw an edge of light come and go at the back of the office and then the man was weaving between the pumps towards them head down against the rain. He came lightly with small hasty steps, so that it was a shock as he crossed in front of the headlights to realise the rolling bulk of his fat.

'Shove your arse over!' Nick started to bump across, but the fat man caught him by the arm. 'Who's this? Stay where you are.'

She watched him cross back in front of the van. The door beside her shook and was dragged open. 'Nice,' the fat man said, studying her. 'Better than your usual anyway.'

As he clambered in, the van sank under his weight so that she fell against him. Sighing as he settled himself, he rolled her thigh under the meaty palm of his hand and said, 'Come to see the fun, have you?' And to the boy, 'Get on with it then. Kite don't want to be kept waiting.'

There was no getting away from so much flesh. At the jerk of her leg he moved his hand, but his thigh stayed hard against the length of hers.

'You know my ambition?' Nick crouched over the wheel squinting ahead. 'I want to be able to speak as good as you Georgie. I mean really take a grip. I'll do it too, I will – on a street corner or in a hall, wouldn't make no difference. Georgie give me a lot of tips,' he explained to her, 'like holding your breath between one streetlight and

187

the next – builds your lungs, makes them strong. In this life you have to go for it, what you want, it's all down to will-power. One night one night soon it's going to come together and I'll have them in the palm of my hand and I'll say to myself tonight I was nearly, nearly Georgie Clarke. But I'll *never* be as good as Kite.' And he turned his head and she thought he was frowning in anger, but he said, 'I know that, Georgie. Not *ever*.'

'Boy's nervous,' the fat man said to her. 'Only natural.'

'Who's nervous?' Nick shrilled.

'Better talking than shitting himself.' And his fat heaved against her in shakes of silent laughter.

Later in what turned out to be a brothel, he explained it to her. She had never been in a brothel before; it had not occurred to her she would ever be in one in her life. If anyone had asked her what one might look like, she would have guessed red flock wallpaper. In fact the walls in this room had been given an emulsion coat in green; under it, though, you could see the raised whorls of the original pattern – so perhaps after all there might have been red under there at one time.

He sat opposite her, spilling over the edges of a little two-seater couch. 'They wasn't anything to do with us – not with Pax,' he explained. 'Some of them were just in having a quiet drink, but everyone round that way hates niggers. And Kite knew, Kite always knows when it matters, that Team would be boozing in there tonight. And they were, just as well they were, or the darkies would have had us, murdering bastards, them's the ones with swords.'

At the time, however, when the van pulled to a stop, she still imagined she was being taken to some kind of political meeting. Behind an iron fence and a surround of tired grass, there was a squat one-storey structure with its windows lit and outer doors lying open. She had attended Free Church services in buildings very much like that. Neither of the men gave any sign of moving. The fancy

188

came to her that if a window was wound down, she might hear the sound of hymn-singing.

'If I wasn't here,' the fat man said, 'two lovebirds, you'd be enjoying yourself, wouldn't you, darling?'

'She's not—' Nick trailed off.

'Not?' He leaned across her and took the boy by the shoulder. 'Not bloody what?'

'She came to the shop tonight.'

The suffocating weight of him moved off her as he sat back. It was as if he was looking at her for the first time. '. . . You from a paper?'

By instinct, Anne moved back from the note of menace. 'She's a friend of Jock the Hat,' the boy said, not sounding at all sure.

'Allander? He talking about Fraser Allander?'

'Not a friend,' Anne said. 'He's one of my patients.'

'That's the first I've heard of it, Georgie!'

'You hold your noise,' the fat man said. '. . . Looks like we're too early. Go over to the boozer and check with Kite.'

They sat in silence watching the boy jerk his way across the street like an ill-hung puppet. The pavement glistened in the light from the public house.

'. . . Jock The Hat.'

'Fraser Allander,' Anne said.

'In to dry out, was he?'

'He was being treated for alcoholism.'

'Where would that be?'

Anne didn't answer. She eased herself across on to the seat the boy had left.

'Did he tell you he was a gunman? He liked to tell people that.'

'Not to me,' Anne said.

'Handing a shooter to a falling-down drunk. You wouldn't want to believe everything he told you . . . anything, really.'

'He told me about Pax Britannica.'

189

'And you came from . . . all the way from . . . wherever you came from. He must have made it sound good.'

One moment the street was empty, the next with heart-stopping suddenness a knot of men burst from the vestibule of the church-like building. In a rearguard action they were driven across the grass and out stumbling and cursing through the gates.

'At last,' the fat man said.

Even in shock, her mind worked sorting out what she was seeing. The group that was being driven back consisted of perhaps a dozen, certainly not more than twenty, white men. They kept close together and they were being attacked by a larger group, twice as many, dark men in turbans, turbans was that Sikhs? wasn't that Sikhs?

'Animals, animals,' the fat man was saying, 'Cowardly bastards.'

Just in front of the van an elderly man in a green turban was shouting and pulling at them, yes, mostly they were young, trying to get them to stop. And yet despite the uproar and the heavy surge of men, she was cool enough to see that it was mostly a matter of threatening, shoving, waving fists, nothing so very bad was happening after all.

The retreat milled to a stop in the middle of the road. Mostly now they seemed to be arguing rather than striking out. On the edge of the group a car inched its way through, hooting derisively as it accelerated clear.

'There's Kite,' the fat man said.

He stood on the other side of the road outside the pub, the boy Nick a head taller behind him. Even at that distance he gave an impression of being dapper, self-contained, the long tight-fitting black coat only emphasising the slightness of him. At his neck there was the white gleam of a shirt and, all her senses heightened, she knew its expense as if fingering folds unfolding of soft heaviness. He stood with his hands by his sides, relaxed, but it wasn't as if he was still. He seemed to give off energy, he vibrated with energy. His face was only an impression to her, wide

190

and big-nosed. It was the stillness of his energy, the energy of that stillness.

And then he stepped forward. Like pulling a cork from the mouth of a jug, men poured from the pub. Dozens of them. Young. Wearing their youth like a uniform. Cropped heads. Scarves like banners. Tumblers swinging like clubs, breaking, slicing like razors. Now there was hurt. And still she couldn't stop, observing, recording. She saw the first group of white men, a moment ago being attacked, rushing to get between the Sikhs and the gate to trap them to their enemies in the open street. She saw the Sikhs understanding suddenly too, trying to fight their way back. She saw the crowd fall on them.

And then she smelled the fat man beside her. He leant forward panting, sweat ran in floods down his cheeks. His hand was between his legs clutching himself. 'Yes,' he cried, 'yes, yes.' In front of them the man in the green turban was tripped and went down. After the first blows he got up on hands and knees. She saw the long pull back of a boot and the swing of it into his face, and again and again. His body lifted to kicks. She knew how vulnerable the brain was in its fragile case of bone.

And then it was over. Only the injured left behind; men scattering.

The door beside her hung open. The fat man was outside. 'No no,' she heard a voice choked with weeping and it was her own. She had to stop him. No more hurting. But when she got to him the fat man was as attentive as a student bent over a book, looking down at the man in the green turban who lay on his back with eyes open, legs trembling spasmodically.

As she knelt at the man's side, a hand gripped her arm and pulled her upright. It was the boy Nick, 'Comeon! moveit! moveit!' He was hysterical with excitement, and when she tried to pull free took a tighter convulsive grip that hurt her. 'Don't mess about stupid cow you want to be here do you?' He dragged her with him to the van, threw her in and followed her into the passenger's side.

'We was almost too late!' The pustule on his nose had burst, and she thought that'll give him relief, and wondered at the oddness of that occurring to her. 'God, if I'd missed it!' In the light from the street she saw there was a smear of blood on her sleeve from his hand. She swallowed and drew a breath against being sick.

With a yell the fat man heaved up into the driver's seat. The door shut and they were moving backwards very fast, reversing round the corner and then forward again, turning right and racing back the way they had come. She was conscious of hands on the wheel, big hands with swollen fingers, and then of his legs filling all the space thrusting against the cloth of his trousers. Their voices echoed, the succulent wheeze of the fat man's mixing with Nick's, making sense to her in fragments. *Magic/left them for dead/ everything went/you see Kite/dead/magic/see Kite standing there/magic/did for one anyway me no problem/like a bleeding general standing there/smooth as silk/magic/dead/Kite see Kite/be proud of us*

'You think we couldn't run the country? Give Kite the chance! ... Not that it's likely. We know. We're not stupid. But, listen, you have any idea how many votes Hitler got in elections? Peanuts that's how many — until the Depression came along that is. Or what about Lenin? People in the caff in Switzerland would have laughed in your face, Kite says, if you'd told them, see that little bald geezer in the corner there? he's going to be the new Czar of Russia. Ha, ha, bleeding hang about till 1914 comes along, laugh then. We're not stupid. "We English are a wonderful people" you know who said that? Mrs Thatcher, that's who. Said that to the Young Conservatives she did. A wonderful people that's us.' The two-seater couch creaked as he rocked back and forward, smoothing the sweat off his forehead, down each cheek in turn.

'Nick told me you lot were good at making speeches,' she said.

'That's politics, isn't it?'

192

'You call what happened tonight politics?'

Talking all the time on a high of excitement, he had brought her and she had gone along not sure what would happen if she refused. She had thought this quiet house was the garage owner's home, but when she said that to him going in the fat man had grinned, 'My wife and daughter will be watching the telly. Wouldn't be fair to disturb them, doctor.'

''Course you could call it politics,' he said, the couch groaning as he shifted from one ham to the other. 'What else I been explaining? But you don't listen. Why? Because you don't care. But I'm supposed to credit you're here because Fraser Allander shot off his mouth about the Pax. So what do you call you turning up here then? A house call?'

His head jerked round at the sound of the door opening. The girl stopped in surprise. She was wearing only white G-string briefs and a bra that looked in need of a wash. Her thighs were long and pale.

'Sorry,' she said.

'I told Doreen we'd be in here,' the fat man said.

'Oh . . . sorry.'

'The dinosaur had a brain in its tail. Like this one,' he said to Anne. 'It takes a while for the message to reach up top.'

Anne hated the casualness of that contempt. She smiled at the girl, who frowned in response and shut the door behind her with as much of a bang as she dared.

'She wants to mind her manners,' the fat man said. 'So you know who I am. Georgie Clarke, I run a garage. And you're Anne, Doctor Anne, right?'

'With a patient called Fraser Allander. Who told me he was a member of Pax Britannica.'

'In good standing – when he could stand. Anyway we've been through that.'

'He came to me because he'd recognised one of the visitors to the hospital. Monty Norman?' deliberately making a question of it.

193

The fat man went very still. 'I knew a Monty. Different second name though.' Nodding at her, he rubbed his hand on his chest, cupping the fat of it like a woman's breast. 'The Monty I knew, well, he was like your patient Fraser, he took off. One night he was in his usual haunts as the law says, next morning he wasn't. Definitely not. It wasn't that people didn't look for him. Some of them looked hard. Some people really wanted a word. He wasn't around any more.'

'Why did he disappear?'

'End of last year. Don't tell me – that's when.'

'You're not interested in why?'

'Where maybe . . . Fraser Allander was sure it was him? Why would he tell you?'

'I told you he was a patient of mine.'

'Fill his prescription, did you? What are you here for?'

She was so tired there was a moment's temptation just to say to him: I'm here because Fraser said the man was able to hypnotise people. And if that is so, then the things on Lucy's tape are not just sick imaginings.

And if he asked again . . .

I'm here because I'm in love. Wasn't that the truth?

'Don't tell me,' the fat man broke into her thoughts. 'It's always love.' And as she stared at him in fright went on, 'Are you the wife?'

Bewildered she said, 'Monty Norman has a wife?'

His mouth turned down like a disappointed child. 'Monty wasn't the marrying kind. Fraser was shit – but some women like shit. Don't tell me, darling, has to be a man, always is.'

He jerked and heaved to his feet. For an endless second she thought he was going to attack her.

'Stay there! Don't even bleeding think about moving!'

The door slammed shut behind him. It seemed unlikely he would have given her a chance to escape without getting someone to stand watch. She had no idea even which district this house was in. Deliberately, she took one slow breath and then another, making it as long as she could manage. House of ill repute she thought, give a thing its name.

So much had happened; exhaustion made her light-headed; it was the way she imagined being drunk must feel. When the fat man came back, the woman who accompanied him was thin. The respectable grey skirt hung from the bones of her hips and the blouse showed hollows in her neck and throat. Jack Sprat, Anne thought, and his Mrs come to lick the platter clean. She bit the inside of her lip, blinking at the pair of them.

'Ask Doreen,' the fat man said.

'I'm sorry?'

'You want to know what your husband came here for, ask Doreen.'

'I'm not married.' She tasted the saltiness of blood on her tongue.

'He comes here because he likes to hurt people,' Doreen said. As she spoke, her upper lip hardly moved. Anne's mother would have called it a refined voice, an attempt at refinement.

'Women,' the fat man said, correcting the definition. 'He likes to hurt women. But I expect you know about that.'

'Who? Who in the world are you talking about?'

He nodded to the woman, who said, 'Mr Rintoul, of course.'

She shook her head. She didn't feel like laughing any more.

'Coming here men'll give you any kind of name – except their own.' It was Doreen's first trace of animation. Most people enjoyed the shop talk of their trade. That was something Anne had noticed. 'Been coming here for, I don't know, three years anyway. He didn't ask for it right out, not the first time, but he knew what he wanted, all right. When little Tracey had to leave, didn't we wonder if he'd be back?'

Doreen turned to the fat man, but he stared fiercely back as if defying her to ask for guidance. It was that, rather than the woman's appeal to him, which put it into Anne's head that he might have money in the place. Perhaps he had set Doreen up in business. There was something in her tone which suggested that as a possibility.

'He was here,' she said, 'well, it wasn't regular, three or four times a year. It was the last time he came I saw him talking to Monty. Out in the hall there. I didn't even know they knew one another.'

'But they used the same girl,' the fat man cried. 'Rintoul and Monty used the same girl. How could I have been such a fool as not to think of that?'

Remembering afterwards, Anne was never sure how real the danger had been. At the time, she was in no doubt. Later she changed her mind one way and the other. Certainly, he had been desperate to find out where Monty Norman could be found. He kept wiping at the sweat on his face, and it burst out, shining along the line of his upper lip as she had seen it in a man recovering from a heart attack. She was in a house where women were hurt, he told her that. And the girl, that happened: Doreen bringing her in; the weals on her. In the toilet, sick, Anne about to sit down stopped to spread paper around the rim under her. The mirror showed her face white, but in her hurry she had left her bag behind and had no make-up to repair her defences. She splashed water on her eyes; then could not bring herself to use the towel. The place was diseased.

Quite soon after that, however, she was being driven back to her hotel. That it was still night disoriented her, so long a time seemed to have passed. 'There we are again,' the fat man said, nodding out of the window. Rain hissed across the forecourt and its hunch-shouldered pumps. 'Monty would come to the garage for me and we'd go on to the meetings together. We were best mates.' He bent his head to squint up at the boiling darkness of the sky. 'He told me the moon was made of ice more likely than not, though the scientists wouldn't ever admit it. And that there had been moons before that one we have now.

196

Six of them, I think it was. One of those old moons came too near and that was when the dinosaurs got so big. All the seas gathered up in a bunch round the equator. Drawn by the moon, you know, just like now. And when it crashed down, well that was what finished off the dinosaurs, wasn't it? And Atlantis as well – or maybe that was one of the moons before that one. You're an educated woman, you'd have been able to go into it with him.'

'If you were such friends—' she began, and stopped in fright. She had no doubt the man beside her was the same one Lucy had described under hypnosis for Doctor Cadell. She had been about to ask how he had escaped the punishment Monty Norman had run from. Had he promised if they spared him he would find his friend for them?

'Some of the best nights of my life talking to Monty.' He sounded wistful, meaty hands clamped on the wheel, thighs sprawling. Then with a change of tone, swinging his head to look at her, 'Your sort don't know it all. Hitler used to talk about the ice between the planets and how the Aryans was led out of Atlantis into Asia – when he was with friends, Monty told me, when he was comfortable like among friends. And Hitler read the books, Monty said. Same books Monty read. He wouldn't talk to Kite about it, Kite would just laugh. I'm not saying I believed it all. But I miss Monty. I'll always miss Monty.'

It struck her he was speaking as if of a man already dead.

In the sanctuary of her hotel room, she lay down on the bed and fell asleep. When she woke, she had no idea where she was. Angling her arm up to check the time, she had to pull back the sleeve of her jacket and realised then she was still fully dressed. It was early, just after seven. She had slept only for a few hours, but slept so deeply her neck cramped when she tried to move. The night before the woman Doreen had said, 'Men come here for what they can't get at home. Mr Rintoul wouldn't have got much from you. You don't like men, do you?' Shop talk again. Experience's half truth; the whore's rationalisation about the faults of wives; should the good wife kneeling hand the sadist the whip? keep your husband happy, like a save-your-marriage article in a woman's magazine, *Cosmopolitan* or one with knitting patterns all the same, women were such fools, and prostitutes as fooled as any it seemed. But could see into you, what you wanted, experience did that for them: every woman to her own trade. 'You're not much interested in men, are you?'

The minute hand on the watch jerked forward. She stretched her arms by her sides and letting her eyes close lay still.

There was a panic when she couldn't find her bag, money, return flight tickets, but it had been handed in at reception. Going through the station to get the train for Heathrow, she held it tight under her arm. It wasn't to be opened to give to the woman begging in the lavatory; or the boy squatted at the foot of the Tube stairs all corners like a creature disjointed, stretching up his hand and startling her with the mechanical croak of his pleading. Hitler had been no older straying out of a Viennese dosshouse to scrounge a copy of a völkisch-occult magazine where he would read of the World Ice Theory and the purity of the Aryan. She found the sight of the boy unendurable. Nothing less than gathering him up in her arms and caring for him would meet his case. She hurried past without opening her purse.

At the airport she bought a paper, and then a copy of half a dozen others. None of them made a mention, not even in the most out-of-the-way paragraph, of the riot she had seen the night before. It was as if it had never happened.

BOOK SEVEN

Screams From the Basement

27

The Tube station had tile walls and seemed to her a very white and open space after the long walk through the tunnels. At the bottom of the first stair two children sat side by side, one not more than four or five, the other older and it was the older one who held out her hand as you came down off the last step and made a plea without words a kind of brief keening, and what were you to do? giving her a coin seemed not enough, nothing enough but gathering them up in your arms and taking them home with you, and you were horrified, disgusted, where was the Fagin hiding? for there had to be one of those, perhaps the two not even sisters, and you went by without giving them anything, not a coin, far less the love that had no thought of self. She saw Anne Macleod on the opposite platform dressed as a man and waved trying to catch her attention, wanting her to wait so that she could run down again through the tunnels and join her; she would tell her about the children. Instead without even glancing up Anne stumbled and spun over. Falling from the platform she made a black cross shape, trousered legs held up as she fell. Her hitting the ground came muffled and a little distant like the sound of blows. And two men ran almost to the edge and then swung off like gulls startled in flight, and both platforms suddenly were filled with people, hands everywhere thrown up to hold back the noise from the tunnel, the roar of the train dazzling from the tiled walls. She was the engine driver rushing into an unfolding openness of mouths stretched wide and hands crying Stop. And in the same moment the wall of the platform was rough against her bruised face and the rail sang by her ear as the train came. And she thought she must be Anne Macleod and then was herself and Anne Macleod's weight lay heavy on her and she was grateful for she was being protected greater love hath no man than this only not a man of course, but then the weight on top of her was moving and thick flesh entered her. Anne was Anne was, *no*, Maitland was inside her. And excitement became fear and turned to anger — why now? couldn't he hear the train, what was the hurry? why now? anyway it was so long since they had anyway it was too late. The driver saw hands held up like posters but there wasn't time or room enough. It was stopping but not ever in time. Brakes shrieked. Maitland thrust into her. The train ground past the place under the soiled wall where she lay held by him. She stood on the platform and watched the train go by and knew she was dreaming and wakened and Maitland thrust and thrust again and groaning let his weight sag down on her.

She struggled to throw him off and he caught her wrists and with his whole weight held her down like an enemy.

'I can't breathe!'

He rolled to the side and in doing so somehow the grip on her changed into a holding for comfort; and she recognised the nature of this change even before he began to make soothing noises which at last resolved themselves into a murmured, 'You were sleeping.'

'Let me go,' she said, and waited until he took his arms away.

'I was sleeping,' she said. 'How could you?'

'It's all right.' He made the mistake of using the same tone, as if calming a child.

'Oh, it's not, no, it's not. Don't think it, it isn't. I was asleep.'

'Yes,' he said.

'You weren't making love to me. Just doing what you wanted. Taking as if I was a thing. Not someone.'

'Oh, for God's sake.' She was, it seemed, trying his patience.

'There's no love in that.'

In all the years they had been married, he had never done this to her. Making love was to someone, not to a body with the spirit elsewhere.

'You could make allowance.'

'What?'

He got out of bed. The curtain was drawn and his naked body before the window seemed to shine in the cold brilliant light. As clearly as if through her own eyes, she saw through his the full moon resting just for a moment on the dark edge of the mountains.

'I almost died this morning,' he said.

Walking up through the woods, ground firm underfoot that had been a sucking of black leaf mould in summer, panting a little from the effort of climbing, she had wanted but not been able to tell Anne Macleod about the phone call. Maitland had been killed.

'They told me you were.'

'I'm sorry.' But he spoke without turning from the window, the shape of him dark against the light. 'I can't imagine who phoned, though.'

'A man.'

'. . . yes.'

'He had an accent, from somewhere in England. That was what confused me. I knew you were going to Aberdeen. But, of course, that was where he was phoning from. A policeman.'

'He said he was a policeman?'

'I think so – I don't know.'

'It's very strange.'

'I don't know what you're saying. That you don't believe me?'

She had been standing at the window when the taxi brought him home near the end of the day. And the heart in her body had melted for joy to see him.

'I thought you were dead. For all those hours,' she said.

'If I'd been asked to guess what you would do on being told I was dead . . . That's a game all of us play in our heads, men do anyway . . . When I play it with you dead, I am grief-stricken, yet brave. Dignified. People are impressed. You, on the other hand, went for a walk. I wouldn't have guessed that.'

'Come back to bed.'

'This place is like a sick-room.'

'I closed the windows and put on the heating. After an accident your body is in shock.'

'It's functioning.'

He turned into silhouette so that she could see the rod of his penis erected from his body.

Feeling him inside her, she wanted to say, I never imagined you dead, not ever, I never played that game.

When he lay by her side, she said, 'There wasn't anywhere for me to go. You were dead. I put down the phone and later I was outside. The odd thing is I'd got dressed for a walk. I'd gloves and boots and a heavy coat and scarf, though I didn't remember putting any of them on. In the woods I met someone who told me your friend Monty Norman is a kind of Nazi.' She waited for him to answer, but he sighed and drew another breath like a man asleep.

He took her again just before morning. This time again she was awake. She had lain awake all night waiting for morning to come.

Finished, the weight of him stretched along her body, he whispered into her ear, 'I killed a child.'

Mysteriously the words connected to no event in her mind but ran instead out into an unknown of possibilities so that it was an easing, before the shock came, when he confined it to the narrow reality of what it was. When his car plunged through that corner it had hit an eleven-year-old girl on a bicycle. The force of the impact threw her forward so that before the car went into the wall it almost struck her again, though by that time she was dead.

She wept for the child and for him. Hardly knowing

what she said offered reassurance. It was an accident, no matter how terrible not his fault.

'The brakes failed,' he said. 'That's what happened and now I've to hope that's what their experts find.'

'Then they will.'

'The front was smashed up. I don't know about these things. Maybe that will make it harder. What do you think?'

She saw the Peugeot with the bonnet sprung open, the lamps emptied out like scooped eggshells. 'I can't bear it. You might have been killed.'

'I wouldn't know how to make the brakes fail. How do you think you would do that?'

'Make them?'

'Make them. Cut something or untighten something. I told you I don't know. But, of course, it would have to take some time. Not much point if they failed coming out of the garage.'

She sat up. 'No one would do that.'

He lay on his back. Only his eyes slid to the side following her.

'Do you remember the time someone put contraceptives into my briefcase? You said the same thing then.' He lay there waiting for her to speak, and she knew it was important to find something to say. After a time, he got up and began to dress. 'Thank God, I hadn't been drinking.' He said that as he was fastening the buttons on a shirt, his tone quite ordinary. And later, slipping his feet into his shoes, 'They call it reckless driving apparently if it comes to a charge. The maximum penalty for reckless driving is five years. A policeman told me that, he said it wasn't enough. Of course, some of them were upset because it was a child. That's natural.'

She wondered if the man who phoned had told her Maitland was dead to punish her. That seemed unfair since she had done nothing. One flesh. Married people all committing masturbation, one flesh. Monty Norman and Maitland. She heard him coming out of the bathroom and going downstairs. Men could love men as women women. Not lovers, the idea foolish as much as sick, rather like a man and his image in the mirror – the image you love or dislike but which is closer to you than any lover – its skin, the dry roughness of gums, the weight of flesh under the eyes, peering out through gaps in its bones at a blurred twin. Maitland looking into a mirror and Monty looking out at him. What would she see if she looked in the mirror?

The idea of her body was strange to her, Maitland had made it strange to her. He had taken her body from her.

28

From the kitchen window the silvery grey elaeagnus bushes hid the bottom of the garden. She listened to the silence in the house. A cup laid aside on the draining board was half full of coffee; when she laid a finger to its side, it was still warm.

Outside the air stabbed at her cheekbones and the hollow of her throat. With Anne Macleod yesterday she had sat under a grey sky, now it was the coldest cloudless blue except for a skein like wool teased out just underneath the sun.

Shivering across the crisp lawn to check if the car was gone, she went all the way round to the front drive. Like a fool, she thought. Hadn't she been told? In a police garage the car would be up on a ramp waiting to be examined. How could she have forgotten? Going back inside, out of habit she took care to reshut the side gate. Lambs and ewes escaped in summer out of the fields, belly-flopping between fence wires. Let them in and they would destroy a garden.

Not expecting to find him, she made her way down past the hedge, not really expecting to find him there, going down anyway; an old lawn of rough grass, the vegetable bed gone to weeds, a garden hut with its rusty padlock snapped to, locking the door shut. Her head blocked the light and the dirt thick on the glass made it hard to see in. As she leant this way and that a piece of the window ledge broke off under her fingers. The hut was rotting into the ground.

They had set a stone into the bank as a foothold up on to the kitchen lawn. As she stepped from it, she saw a face at the window, only a glimpse, so quick it might not have been there at all and then certainly it wasn't. It had to be Maitland. Who else? She hesitated at the back door, left unlocked when she came out.

A hand fell on her right shoulder.

Part of her fright was superstition, for it was as if whoever had been at the window had conjured himself behind her.

Stepping back Monty Norman gave her fear room. 'I saw you come round to the front of the house,' he said, 'so I knew somebody was in.'

She said, 'He isn't dead, if that's why you've come.'

Later it occurred to her that if she had kept silent, he might have given himself away. But now by what she had said he was warned. Yet she could not have stopped the words and later would not regret them for it was by thinking about them afterwards that she began to understand what they had come from her own mouth to tell her.

When he followed her inside, there was no one in the kitchen. She took the empty cup from beside the sink and ran it under the tap. Behind her she could sense him standing too close. Maitland might have gone out walking; if so, there was no way of telling when he would come back. Or he might have gone to work, that wasn't impossible, caught a bus into Balinter and gone to the University. The water spilled over the side of the cup.

His hand reached over her shoulder and shut off the tap. In the silence there was the sound of a door closing. She knew at once it must be the lavatory at the end of the passage by the front door and knew, even before Maitland appeared, that he would be carrying a magazine or book. It had not occurred to her that he would reassert the routine of any ordinary morning.

He came into the kitchen reading aloud, 'Those of us in industry who have the privilege of leadership—' He stopped short. 'That's the bit I like,' he went on, drawing the words out, staring at Norman.' "The privilege of leadership".' He glanced down at the folder open in his hand. ' "Those of us in industry who have the privilege of leadership should not leave the destiny of our country solely in the hands of politicians". I thought I might use it in a seminar.' And with no change of tone, 'Are we having breakfast? Suddenly I'm hungry.'

They ate breakfast sitting at the table and Lucy made it. She put muesli into a bowl and set it down in front of Maitland who poured on honey then milk. Monty Norman shook his head, not wanting any. She grilled bacon and made toast and not just coffee as usual but tea as well since that was what their guest asked for. She didn't feel at all like eating and when they were served she poured herself a coffee and sat at the table too. Part of her felt it as strange. But she did it. What sense would it have made to feel demeaned by something as everyday as making breakfast?

Afterwards though when the two men went out together, she began in her head to describe all of it to Anne Macleod. What words would she find to tell how she had made a breakfast eaten in silence and then how the two men had gone out leaving her? She sat looking from Maitland's bowl where he had pushed it aside to the two plates, crumbs, a fragment of crust. She began to gather the dishes together as if in a moment she would take them to the sink for washing.

And having got so far with Anne Macleod would she be able to find the words for that too? Just say it. Washed them. And then?

She got up and went into the hall. Moving more quickly all the time, she put on her coat and a hat. Not able to find the second glove, she stuck one hand in her pocket and hurried out by the back door leaving it unlocked again behind her.

Turning left, she couldn't pick out a car that might be Norman's. The scatter parked on either side seemed the familiar early morning pattern of the village street. On the other hand, it had to be said she was capable of trying to get the key in the lock of a different make from their own simply because the colour was the same, more or less the same, and so that didn't prove much. His car might still be there and the two men walking somewhere nearby.

She could go back down through the woods towards the estate as she had done yesterday. Or to the top of the Brae Road. From there on a day like this she would be able to look across all the counties of the strath.

With telescope, searching: unwanted, Lucy Inside gave her that image.

'I was watching you from inside the shop.' The minister's wife tapped her on the arm with her newspaper. 'Standing in a dream.' She started to walk, drawing Lucy into step beside her. 'The manse is finally sold, isn't it wonderful? An offer of sixty thousand. Believe me, they'll have to spend that much again to get rid of the damp. I can't tell you how glad David and I shall be to move. Did you know it has to be to a four-bedroom house? Not that we need so much. There's a church rule – bedrooms for children and you need one for the visiting minister. All out of date – nineteenth century, eighteenth, seventeenth, *some* century or other. All nonsense, in any case. Any century but this one.'

It was Janet's house they were passing. This morning would she be curled up in a chair head bent over a book about women opening their legs? Perhaps now she didn't have to. At the gable end there was a lane and Lucy turned into it. Behind her she heard the minister's wife rattle on for half a sentence before coming to a stop. She was a woman who was fonder of talking than listening. Poor Lucy, she'd say, still behaving rather oddly I'm afraid.

Madness had its privileges.

On this side of the street the village was as wide as a single house, each one with a garden so long that it seemed narrow; feus from a time when land was cheap. The burn of brackish water that wound along behind them was stilled in ice, and late autumn's sucking churn of mud

210

beside it had frozen into a path. Cold weather had taken a grip just when it was time to think of the way things would be when spring came back.

They were no more than half a mile ahead when she came in sight of them, but beginning to hurry she made no impression, even after a bit seeming to fall further behind. It would be Maitland, she knew, setting the pace. I should call out, she thought; and then, What would happen if I called: Mr Clarke! Would Monty Norman turn round? If I called, Your friend Georgie Clarke is here! – but she wouldn't have the courage. Anyway they had stopped, heads together, now were moving on, but more slowly, lingering along. In a moment, they would hear her footsteps or one of them would look round. The sound of her breath hurried in her ears.

'Mr Rintoul!' she called.

She wakened out of a dream and it was dark. It wasn't a frightening dream just strange, and she lay under the weight of her husband's arm piecing it together and then thinking about how the two men had turned and that the name she had called out might have been heard by them as 'Maitland!'

People heard what they expected to hear, she knew that.

Stumbling in her haste over the rutted track, she had begun a sort of apology as soon as she was near enough. 'I didn't think you would come this way. The woods are still muddy, of course, though it's so cold. I couldn't stay indoors.'

The men had been walking side by side, but the track was too narrow to take three abreast. Maitland had her and Norman go in front of him. His voice from behind them said, 'Alfried Krupp had a torture chamber in the basement of the company's headquarters.' When she looked round, he smiled at her. 'I'm talking about during the war, of course.'

Talking about the war. If that was all! Past history.

Between shoulder-high banks like walking down the bed of a ditch, they came to a place where they were forced out on to the frozen surface of the burn. Maitland was wearing heavy walking shoes with ribbed soles that let him step confidently. He took her by the arm. Beside them, Monty Norman's thin-soled city shoes slid under him treacherously.

'Did you ever hear that speech by Oswald Mosley — "there comes a time in the lives of great nations?" Those extraordinary snarling vowels ranting on about destiny. They tell me street-corner orators are spouting that stuff again. Don't you find that extraordinary?' As he spoke, she watched the breath puff from his mouth like the white smoke that came with each boom from a cannon. 'That conference hand-out reminded me of it. A sentence like that is a collector's item. "Those of us in industry, the privilege of leadership." And for syntax as much as semantics. How much of a balance sheet do you need before you can get away with talking about "destiny"? Without anybody laughing, I mean?'

'Laughing? how far before we get back to the road?' Monty Norman ran the two questions into one. He hates this, Lucy thought.

'Not far. Or instead of "laughing" you might as well say "weeping". Did you know the SS contracted to provide labour from Auschwitz to Siemens? Not just the lamp-shades were made of skin in those days, eh? And BMW got *its* workers supplied from Dachau. The camp at Dachau. In the Thirties the Party used to run trips to Dachau for the industrialists — a way of saying thanks for your help — picnics on the grass. And I. G. Farben was so hard on its slaves that the SS complained — they told the directors, Please, the supply isn't infinite. Infinity — another big word. Do you think businessmen use it too, like "destiny"? Without laughing, I mean. Heads held high. Jowls quivering. Wouldn't you think so?' In the way she knew so well, he leaned across her with a little bark of interrogation. 'Hmm?'

212

'Like you say, there was a war on.' Badgered into responding, Monty Norman spat out the words in a nasal whine, his accent quite altered.

And Maitland had stopped, pulling her to a halt with him, and thrown back his head laughing. ' "A war on!" ' he mimicked. 'A war on ... My mother said the village grocer in those days made the women stand in line, grumbled at them, shut up shop when the notion took him, quite apart from overcharging. She got so angry one day, she said to him, Wait until the war's over, no one will come near you then. War over, he said, do you think I'll bloody well be here when the war's over?'

She had heard him like that often, she told herself, ideas in a spate like drunkenness as he jumped from one to the other. And on the other hand – for something was wrong, this wasn't like those other times, however much you might want to pretend it was – my God, hadn't he almost died?

At one point: 'The air's full of lies. We're surrounded by them, swimming in them. Lies and half truths. And euphemisms like candy to sicken you on sweetness. You get sick with longing for the unvarnished this-is-so. If I was in advertising I'd have a picture of a tramp on a bench staring at two Andrex toilet rolls, one wrapped on the bench, the other draped over it. And I'd put the caption: "Bums love them." '

At another: 'Benjamin Lee Whorf who had a hypothesis. A Choctaw Indian could only see the world in one way because of the structure of tenses he had. Language made the world. Take that too literally – some do – and reality would be what we think it is. The crew of a flying saucer looking down one morning and seeing the whole world dislimn – Ben Nevis and Tibet levelling down into the plain and the sand moistening under the Bedouin, till everywhere is much the same – and one little green man turns to the other and says, Oh, oh, they've all learned Esperanto, *big* mistake.'

213

And at another: 'Freud practised hypnotism, did you know that? Eh?'

'Yes, as a matter of fact.'

'I thought you might. He came from Vienna.'

'Yes.'

'Like Hitler. Another hypnotist.'

'If you say so.'

'At the headquarters of Krupp Industries, the secretaries on the fifth floor could hear the screams from the basement.'

And this time Monty Norman hadn't answered, losing his balance as he slithered on the smooth surface of the burn, hating all of this. Without thinking she put out her hand to steady him when he seemed about to fall. As he pulled away – her instincts always always out of place – she saw under their feet folds of lank grass as leached under the ice as drowned child flesh might be.

All right at first, after an hour or so out of bed she realised she was cold. Something had gone wrong with the heating. Nothing happened when she turned the thermostat valves to full on the radiators. In the cupboard under the stairs the Potterton box showed both lights on at red, for hot water and central heating. In the garage apart from the little blue lick of the pilot light there was no flame under the boiler. She went back for a jersey and gloves and then outside to where the grey Calor gas tank bulked awkwardly placed at the side of the house. The padlock on the gauge cover wouldn't work loose and she took off her gloves to fiddle with it.

By the time it wrenched free she was almost weeping with the pain of her fingers, numb and white at the tips. The gauge showed the tank still a quarter full.

Her first thought was of Maitland who had been collected by Sam Wilson after breakfast and carried off to Balinter for a faculty meeting. To disturb him with a call for help: it was the kind of thing you had to do at once without a thought, otherwise it seemed too feeble. She could phone an electrician or a plumber; a heating engineer assuming it was the boiler that had gone wrong; there was no one in the village though. Weren't you supposed to have them serviced? Maitland should have seen to it.

There was an electric fire stored at the back of the garage for throwing out. The first thing was to get warm. She carried it into the living-room, panting with the unexpected weight of it. Switched on it fizzled and gave off a smell of frying dust. She put on both bars and the convector for immediate warmth, and then filled the basket in the hearth with paper screwed up to burn slowly. As the flames ran up through them she added sticks and sat on her heels watching until it was time to lay two split logs on top.

In here at least would be warm.

Climbing upstairs, she could tell on her skin how little time it had taken for the heat to drain out of the house. Just behind the door in Maitland's study, a shelf of the bookcase had been cleared for the answerphone and a calendar and phonebooks and a clutter of papers. She sifted through them without finding the list of tradesmen that was usually kept by the phone in the kitchen. The shutter cover of Maitland's desk was rolled down and she hesitated about opening it; but more papers were distributed along the flat top and she had a look through them. Even that felt uncomfortably like snooping.

About to leave, she noticed the tell-tale light on the answerphone signalling a message. She had been so intent on her search she hadn't noticed it before. Smiling at that she pressed the play button. The light flickered as the tape ran back then a woman's voice spoke.

'Maitland,' the woman's voice said, 'it's Beth. Don't die of surprise or anything but I've been offered an exhibition in Edinburgh. I want you there. No excuses. Ring me the first chance you get. Love you.'

When it finished she pressed the stop button to keep the message and then played it once more; and again. She was about to listen to it for the fourth time when she heard the ringing of the doorbell.

'I was on the point of giving up,' Janet said, moving forward into the hall. Her cheeks were flushed with the cold and as she came in she tugged off the wool ski cap and shook out her hair. That gesture, the mane of red hair swinging loose, reminded Lucy of something, someone, a stirring of memory, so tenuous yet bitter as death, gone before she could grasp it.

'The back door isn't locked.' That was stating the obvious. It was the way things were in the village.

Janet frowned as if at a diversion. 'I didn't think.'

She wanted it to be like this, the thought came to Lucy, at the front door, ringing the bell like a stranger. She hasn't come as a friend. All the more necessary to treat her as if she had.

Yet the moment went by for that, and it was Janet tired of waiting who led the way into the kitchen.

'We can't stop in here,' Lucy said, coming no further than the doorway.

Janet looked at her in silence, then took a seat at the table.

'Why not?'

She spoke as if issuing a challenge.

'Don't you feel the cold?' And it was cold. Become cold so quickly that she could see her breath as she spoke. 'The heating's gone off. I don't know what's gone wrong with it.'

'Yes.' Janet glanced around. 'Yes . . .' For the first time she seemed uncertain.

'Can't stay here,' Lucy said again. Surely it should be plain to her it would be better if she went?

'You've a smudge,' Janet touched her own cheek with a finger, 'of soot or something.'

'I was lighting the fire.' That was an admission. She had looked at her hands and, yes, they were dirty, licked the side of a knuckle and begun scrubbing her cheek clean when the admission slipped out. That was stupid. Anyway

216

the words once said, there seemed no choice but to go on, '. . . In the living-room. We could go in there.'

'Hmm. Let's.'

As they came out of the kitchen, Lucy indicated by a touch the picture hung in this darkest corner of the hall.

'Do you like this?'

Janet had moved past her and, turning, seemed still poised to go on.

'Like it? Is it new?'

'No. No . . . Maitland used to have it in his study.'

Four potatoes on a rumpled cloth, a dull-seeming thing, a study made with a dark palette. Certainly it might have been easy to overlook; it made no obvious demands.

'Can we get on?' Janet asked, and shivered, seeming to say, It's cold, as if by way of explanation. Apology? If it was a sign of weakness, it was the only one she gave.

'Maitland bought this just before we were married. Such a beautiful day, oh, how the sun shone. The art students had hung their paintings on the railings at the Botanical Gardens. They did that in Glasgow then. What seems strange is that a day like that, all bright colours, flowers and girls' dresses, sunlight in floods, should be tied to a dull thing like this. Beth, her name was Beth. We heard she had died.' With one hand she straightened the painting, making the smallest of adjustments. 'Isn't it strange how we stop seeing things? There they are right in front of our noses. We don't see them. Maitland told me she was dead.'

But Janet was gone, and by the time she went into the front room had taken her stand back to the fire waiting for her.

'It's quite warm,' Lucy said. Janet nodded, one sharp jerk of her chin. 'It's the heater, it's very efficient. Once the fire is properly caught this place will be like an oven.'

'I have to talk to you.'

'Too warm or too cold. Isn't it always the same? I think it's too soon to put the heater off yet, don't you?'

217

'I'm sorry you haven't been well, but things can't go on like this.'

'But you always have something. When you come, I mean.'

'What?'

'You always have something. Tea, coffee, something to drink?'

'No, Lucy, not today.'

Lucy went anyway to the sideboard and found a bottle – the first one that came to hand. From the upper shelf she lifted out two little tumblers. 'Because it's been so cold. It's too cold to go back into the kitchen. So I suppose that's an excuse. We'll have a glass of—' She had to stop and glance at the bottle. 'It's gin. What's best with gin? Tonic, of course. We do have, yes,' she bent to search and came up with a small bottle of Schweppes, 'we can spoil ourselves, just for this once, since it's not an ordinary morning, I still have to phone, for help . . .'

But as she began to take the cap off the bottle of gin, behind her Janet said, 'Why don't you leave him?'

'Last night,' Lucy said pouring the gin into the glasses in turn, trying to judge it, not wanting to ask Janet if it was enough or too much, 'I had the oddest dream. The thing is I don't – well, I know everybody does, but most times I don't remember, they say it has to do with how quickly you wake up.' She added the tonic water to Janet's and then stood with the bottle over her own glass, not pouring. It was always Maitland who made the drinks. 'I was standing on the road outside these high walls, brown not grey, you might have thought they would be grey, and a double door big enough to let in a bus but it was closed. And a little door by the side opened and a man came out. This is the prison, he said. But the poor prisoners – I was crying – there must be thousands and thousands of them. It was such an enormous place. Oh, no, he said, there never has been a prisoner, not ever one since it was built. Just that it's there, that's quite enough, you see.'

She decided against adding anything and took a mouthful of neat gin.

'This isn't any good,' Janet said, 'you have to face up to things.'

Still there, Lucy thought, as she turned round, in front of the fire legs spread I thought it was only men did that getting whatever heat was going, I was hoping she'd gone. Face up to her then, for what it's worth.

'We didn't want it to happen, neither of us did.'

'Does Maitland know you're here?' Obviously not.

'We're in love.'

'Lovers, do you mean?'

'In love too. That's the truth, and it won't change however sorry we are.'

'Sorry for me, you mean.' She went to sip again from her glass but it was emptied.

'It wasn't something we ever wanted to happen. But it has and nothing can change it now.'

'Sorry for me because I was your friend?'

'We want to be together, Lucy.'

Lucy thought about that. She realised she hadn't given Janet the gin and tonic she had poured for her. Picking it up, she drank it herself.

'If you leave Ewen, you may miss him more than you think. Maitland isn't a wife beater.'

'For God's sake!' Janet cried, 'can't we be decent? We've been friends. I don't want that to stop.'

Lucy stared at her in astonishment. As far as the eye could tell, she gave every appearance of being serious. It must be all those books she's been reading, she thought, they've rotted her brains.

'To be fair to Maitland,' she said, 'although you couldn't really call him violent, he has just killed a child.'

From what followed, it could be gathered among other things that Janet hadn't heard of this, which proved nothing except that in the forty or so hours since getting back after the accident Maitland hadn't been in touch with her. Which, again, proved nothing. She seemed to think it might though. Which perhaps proved something.

Left alone again, Lucy went back upstairs at once. She pressed the play button on the answerphone and waited as the light flickered and the tape rewound.

'Maitland,' the woman's voice said, 'it's Beth. Don't die of surprise or anything but I've been offered an exhibition in Edinburgh. I want you there. No excuses. Ring me the first chance you get. Love you.'

Love you.

Sun in the park and Maitland running hand in hand with her across the grass to where railings were made over into a summer gallery and the painters, the young painters – but the world was young then – and Maitland smiling at the girl: *Yes! five whole pounds! though we can't afford it.*

Since we're going to be married! Lucy had cried.

We're investing in you, we're investing in your talent. And she had never forgotten the wonderful look which the girl, in the miracle of her talent and being young, had given him when he said that to her. *This is our investment of faith in you.*

He could make that kind of promise and be believed.

He was Maitland then . . .

If she had got Maitland, there was no telling what she might have said, but in the message she left for him with Sam Wilson only the heating had failed.

It was typical of the little man that he should turn up on her doorstep, where she kept him as he explained that not being able to find Maitland and being so concerned by the idea of her alone in an unheated house in this awful weather he'd made his mind up at last that quite the best thing would be to come himself. And here he was . . . Whatever his faults, he was good-hearted.

It was typical of him, too, that when she relented and let him inside he had stared reproachfully from the log fire roaring in the hearth to the bowl of soup laid out for her lunch and taken off his coat with the air of a man waiting for an apology.

Afterwards, when she could bring herself to think about the things that happened later, it did seem some part of the blame might be laid to him. If he hadn't come, if he had been different when he did, she would have stayed where she was until Maitland returned. To be fair, he had argued against taking her to Balinter. There was no guarantee Maitland would be there; perhaps he had gone off to hire a car; probably he was on his way home right now. Didn't that make sense? Wilson wondered.

Plainly, the chivalric impulse was exhausted.

In the car he drove without speaking, presumably to show how displeased he was, but after a while the silence got to be too much for him. 'It might have been better if Maitland hadn't come at all to the meeting.'

'What?'

'This morning. It was, quite honestly, it was a disaster.'

About money, their meetings now were always about money. He's the first professor I've ever seen come into a meeting with a Filofax, Maitland had said of a new colleague; bids for projects, zero funding options, it's a new language. The afternoon was taut with a washed clean light and to her left where the country was flat she saw the fields like faded rugs thrown down under the hills.

'I know you take an interest,' he was saying.

'Sorry?'

'Perhaps I was wrong. I thought you took an interest. In the Department, the University, what is happening.'

'Not when it's about money.'

'Too *depressing*? Well, of course it is. We waste endless time on whether we can afford to do things, so that all the important questions about why we do them and how we do them, there's no *time* for them at all.'

Talk like this, she had heard it before, for years now. Because he seemed to expect a reply, she offered, 'I know', and sighed.

221

'Oh, *quite*. We're all weary of it. It's part of the grey fabric. But it's the real world we have to live in and we have to cope with it. We can't just give up. That's not *duty*.'

'Duty.'

'You say it exactly the way Maitland would. I'm sorry. I didn't mean that the way it sounded.' She said nothing, not caring; but he wasn't any good with silences. 'The thing is I know how splendid he can be when he's making fun of something. But he *used* to care as well.'

'Henney Low,' Lucy said. He turned his head sharply as if to check whether she was making fun of him. 'Someone Maitland talks about. A clever man who doesn't really care.'

'He was witty this morning,' Sam Wilson, 'but it didn't go down well. It didn't *help*.'

'I've changed my mind,' Lucy said. 'Let me out at the station, would you, please?'

'If you're not feeling well – if you have a headache? – I could take you home again.'

'No.'

Parking at the station entrance, he broke their silence. 'Despite – I mean, I have great respect for Maitland. The work he's done. That doesn't alter. And, of course, it's not surprising if he wasn't at his best – wasn't himself this morning – not after the accident.'

'Killing the child, you mean?'

But she could see from his expression Maitland hadn't mentioned that. She hadn't meant to be disloyal.

The headache started on the train. Just an ordinary headache, not the kind that was an affliction. For those it had been a long time, not one all the nights she had been in hospital. Suddenly that seemed strange to her and she caught herself rubbing at her temple in the old way until she brought the culprit hand into her lap and held it there. She closed her eyes. Opened them at once. A line of bare trees. She watched them and thought of stick men flickering by in a picture book under a child's thumb.

She made her way from the train into the booking hall. With the crowd swirling round her, after all she couldn't find a reason to be in Edinburgh. On the board there was a departure due that would take her back to Balinter. What she needed was a quiet place to be alone. She couldn't make up her mind what to do, and saw she was being watched by a man on one of the ugly plastic seats scarred with cigarette burns. An unshaven man with the battered look of hard times, two plastic bags held between his feet, he watched her as if for a sign.

There were no telephone books at the line of phones under the departure board. She had to walk along to the central post office at the east end of Princes Street. I must speak to Doctor Anne Macleod, she told the answering voice. It's very important.

The clock on the tower of the Balmoral Hotel read quarter to four. She couldn't remember if she had eaten for breakfast or lunch. And there had been the gins when Janet came. Little wonder she had a headache. Nothing more natural.

She took the glass lift down into the shopping mall by the station. After she had eaten something, she would phone again. I'll phone again, she had said. Please tell Doctor Anne Macleod I'm in Edinburgh.

Later her headache was worse and she couldn't recall whether or not she had eaten in the food court. Instead she remembered the way the tables were set out by the pool and the shape the fountain made as it rose and the drops from it falling in circles into the water below. When she found herself in the pedestrian precinct the first thing she took account of was how one of the bushes in the concrete pots had buds, though so tiny and tight you might not notice and think it was dead. After that she looked in the travel agent's window at brown bodies running hand in hand into the sea on another planet. Yellow sand, blue sea, meeting at an edge. By then she

223

knew, of course, that the entry beside the agent's led up to the office of the Gregory and Rintoul Trust.

As she climbed to the Trust office, a young woman ran down the last flight towards her. The impression of a moment; but for an instant, young, full of life, seeing her in that place, it had been Sophie Lindgren.

Slowly she began again to mount the stairs. Hadn't she been promised nothing was certain? Not even the coming of pain.

When she came down across the Meadows, the great open grass space and the arch of sky overhead was like water to her after the noise of the streets. The beauty of the place was its trees; it would be bleak without them; but there were empty gaps on either side of the path where there should have been new saplings. One late survivor must have been attacked only the night before; the slender trunk snapped and bent over like a crippled dancer.

Recognising the street, she crossed the road on impulse and when she had knocked for some time, a man not much more than a boy opened the door.

'The Norman fellow's not in,' he said, sounding rude although that might only have been because of his accent, Belfast and abrupt.

'All the same . . . I've done too much walking . . . I'll have to sit down.'

'I don't suppose he'll be long,' the young man said, taking it all as a matter of course. 'I'm watching television in the kitchen.' He gestured and when she was inside shut the door and started ahead of her along the lobby. 'It's the only warm bit in this hole. And you could have a cup of tea.' After all he was friendly. 'Might make you feel better.' Kind. 'I should be painting,' he was saying, 'but it's hard some days. I can't make myself get started.'

She remembered the kitchen, just as untidy, the tap still dripping. The only difference was the small portable television among the dishes piled beside the bread bin, an unwashed plate on top and a kitchen chair set in front of it. 'It's not really wasting time,' the young man said. 'It's

224

like an Expressionist painting – all shot in the studio. That's Emil Jannings on there now. He's the professor. He's in love and it's driving him mad. He can still bring a tear to your eye. Mind you so can Fräulein Dietrich murdering one of those songs of hers – assuming that is you're a music lover.'

'Is that for me?' He had run a cup under the tap and now was shaking it dry. 'If I could wait in his room. All I need is to be quiet.'

She had hardly got herself seated when he startled her by bursting in with the cup held out. 'Get this down you. It'll help. Can't stop – don't want to miss the end.' And he was gone. A growling version of 'Falling in Love Again' faded along the corridor.

Most of the room was taken up by a bed. It was a comfortless place. The top sheet was drawn up over the bed. She sat on a chair against the wall looking at the bed. To lie down on it and close her eyes. Side by side under a chest of drawers, there was a pair of black shoes and another of brown. Tidy, she thought. No mirror. Nothing on the walls except a calendar. For the wrong date. Not for this year. Some previous occupant might have pinned it there. She was cold.

The ringing of the bell didn't concern her. He would have a key. There were footsteps and the raising of voices at the bedroom door and then it opened and the young Irishman said, 'I told you he's not, but look for yourself.'

The man's face had been put together but you could see the places it had been broken. There was something wrong around the eyes and at one side of the mouth there were little seams like the marks of frowning where the skin had been patched. He stared at her and then went back out and there was the noise of doors being flung open all along the corridor. At one point he said something and the young Irishman stopped protesting, so that after that there was only the sound of the doors.

He came back on his own and stood looking at her. 'This isn't your room?'

225

'No.' Somewhere behind her vagueness the idea offended her.

'You live in this flat?'

'No.' But this time as he waited she knew that wasn't enough. 'Have you made a mistake?'

'That's what I'm trying to find out.'

He opened the wardrobe and she glimpsed a jacket and some shirts on hangers and thought, so there is one, seeing the mirror fixed to the back of the door. He went through the chest of drawers, lifting clothes out and putting them back in place. When he had finished, nothing in the room looked disturbed.

'Mr Nobody, not even a letter.' When he spoke, only the undamaged side of his mouth moved. 'What's he look like, describe him for me.'

She made a movement of denial. He had no right to question her. She should get up and leave.

He put his hand under her chin pushing her head back.

'I can't tell you why I'm here, I don't know why!'

Squinting against the dazzle of light, she saw him nod as if understanding something. 'For Christ's sake! he fixes you up, isn't that right? When you're poorly.' He let her go. 'It has to be him.'

Hearing her come out, he turned. He was already at the outside door ready to leave.

'You were one of them,' she whispered.

'What?'

'Only they punished you.' He came at her in a rush. 'That's what happened to your face.' In her terror he seemed to fill the corridor. 'They ruined me, you said.'

And he had her by the shoulders. 'He tell you that?' She shook her head. 'Or Georgie Clarke – did he tell you?' She struggled but he was too strong, forcing her back easily into the room. No one had told her. A final shove sent her staggering back, and he had her down on her back across the bed. He forced his knee between her legs.

She had heard it on a tape, and hearing it had thought it something invented out of her own mind's darkness.

Perhaps it was the look on her face then that made him stand back. He touched his tie and then made the gesture of a man checking his flies.

'Tell you all about it, did he? Don't laugh, I still fucking dream about it. It was the best time I ever had. Not an old piece of meat, a piece of garbage – in a nothing drum like this. He must be desperate for it, darling.'

She closed her eyes. Would not open them to let him exist, until the voice of the young Irishman told her he was gone.

'Don't touch me,' she said.

'There wasn't anything I could do, honest to God. Sorry . . . Do you want tea?'

It was no wonder Doctor Cadell had felt disgust for what he had found in her mind. He couldn't admit how he felt, of course, any more than a surgeon could acknowledge the part of him sickened by the soft corruptions scooped out under his hand. He hadn't been able to hide what he truly felt, not from her, no matter how he deceived himself. It would be no wonder he felt disgust for her, for the dirty thing pieced together out of the scraps in her mind. Only now the scarred man had laid his hands on her and pretended they were real. Doctor Cadell like Daddy had sent her into the dark.

Yet when she got outside she stood waiting at the entrance to the close, as if something prevented her from going away, and that was where Anne Macleod found her.

29

With a shudder she brought up a last slick of vomit at the side of the road.

When she got back in, Maitland put the car into gear, twisting round to check there was a gap in the traffic as they moved off the hard shoulder on to the motorway. At once he was driving very fast, pulling out to overtake, braking as they closed on a car in front. Perhaps it had been that which made her sick. She found a tissue and wiped her lips; it made no difference to the taste in her mouth. After they had been married for some years one thing or another she had said started him quarrelling with her so badly he had raised his fist. He hadn't struck her, instead appalled by his own gesture had become subdued as if wanting her sympathy, so that she would see how much she was to blame for reducing him to such a state. You have more strength than me, she had said, it's a temptation to use it, I can see that. And that reply had driven him into a second rage: she 'didn't understand'. She had been sick then too.

It was a long time since they had quarrelled about anything.

It had been all right while Anne Macleod was still there. He had settled her into a chair, given her a drink to sip, told her to close her eyes. To the things Anne Macleod said, he had listened quietly. He was calm, so that he was the one who seemed to be in control. Listening without interruption, while she told the story of a man calling himself Rintoul who had used a brothel in London to satisfy appetites he was ashamed of. Suppose, Anne Macleod said, someone who knew about Rintoul needed to find a place to hide. Wouldn't Rintoul have been forced, for example, to find that person a place to live or, assuming he had one in his gift, even some kind of job?

Lucy, closing her eyes as if to deny her own presence, had waited for him to say, What is this to do with me? After a silence, not any longer than you gave someone out of courtesy to make sure they were finished, Maitland thanked her for bringing his wife home; I was beginning to worry, he said.

Would it worry you that she was with Monty Norman? Anne Macleod had asked.

If she spoke at all, Lucy knew she would hear herself tell them about the scarred man. She must have made some kind of noise for Anne Macleod had bent over her, touching her on the shoulder to comfort her, saying, Come with me, you can come away with me now, this moment if you want to. With eyes closed Lucy heard Maitland tell her it was time to go; my wife is unwell, he had said, not sounding angry at all, she needs to sleep.

She wakened some time just after first light. Leaning up on one elbow, he continued to look at her for a while in silence, then he said, I was trying to remember one time when you offered the first move before we made love. Or you ever touching me down there. Unless I asked you to. He lay down and she couldn't see his face when he said, I know it has as much to do with me as you. Maybe if we'd had children.

After that since he didn't say any more he had probably gone back to sleep, but now as she thought about what he had said during the night she knew that somewhere in her there was anger. It was very strange to know it was there and not be able to feel it.

'I was on the phone,' Maitland said.

She couldn't make sense of that, and then she wasn't sure if she had heard him properly. She had been looking at how the white of a cloud of mist linked the snow-covered tops of two hills. Behind them low in the winter sky the sun was small and moon-coloured.

'I was on the phone when you and Doctor Macleod came last night,' he said. 'I couldn't think who the call was from. I didn't recognise the voice. She asked me if I had any children. It's late for a survey, I said. But at that exact moment it came into my head who she must be. If you had any, she said, you wouldn't have killed mine. You couldn't have been so careless, not knowing how precious they are.'

'How could she do that?'

She meant how was the woman able to talk at all: if a child of mine had died under the wheels of a car I would have drowned in tears. But Maitland said, 'That policeman didn't like me much. Not that there's the smallest chance of proving he told her, if it was him.'

It seemed to her that in one way the mother had been brave. Thinking about that, she remembered the day she had hurried along the frozen burn calling 'Mr Rintoul!' She saw the picture of herself doing that, hurrying after the two men, as if she had been a watcher standing somewhere apart on a hill.

'Anyway she didn't threaten me or anything.' Maitland braked and caught a gap that took them into the traffic on the first roundabout before the city. 'Of course, I did put the phone down before she was finished – when I heard the noise of the two of you coming in.'

The mist shrank and bent the light of the headlamps. The locals called it haar, a word for a raw wind across the German plains, a word the old tribes had brought with them when they came north. It poured up off the water of the firth to fill the city. Out of the car, she shivered at its touch. 'Easier to park here and walk across,' Maitland said.

Her heart sank at the effort needed to walk across the links. Out in the middle of the open grassy space, it was hard to believe a city lay round them. She heard the hurry of her breath and their footsteps tapping on the frozen path. Trees came and went singly as stripes of darkness. From somewhere on their left a wordless yelling rose and fell silent. She wanted to sink down, but Maitland took her by the arm. She could not think why he had chosen to park so far away.

When she thrust her hand into her pocket, there were no gloves, she must have left them in the car. Instead, she found a bottle, a small square shape that she turned over and over between her fingers.

'I don't want to do any harm,' she said, 'to you or him.'

As they entered the street, he didn't answer. Perhaps she had only thought the words. In the ground-floor flats uncurtained windows showed long narrow kitchens fiercely lit or square shadowy rooms in glimpses, pictures, mirrors, a television set in a corner. As they went into the close, he said, 'There is no me and him. Isn't that what we're here to prove?'

Climbing the stair took an enormous effort. All the feeling seemed to have gone from her legs. Waiting for the bell to be answered, she was afraid she would fall down. Her hand clenched on the bottle, squeezing it in her fist. They waited so long it began to seem no one would come and he would have to take her home so that she could sleep. She saw him take out a ring with two keys on it. First he used the Yale and then with the long thin key turned the lock below that and pushed the door open.

She knew him so well. And part of what she knew was that less than anyone in the world would he be able to endure her seeing him as the poor shameful thing that was Rintoul. He was taking her to Monty Norman who would hypnotise her into forgetting everything. Why else would he have keys? The idea frightened her, but if giving her their life back was a matter of forgetting, she would forget and be grateful to forget.

Why had he parked the car so far away?

Sitting on the same chair in Monty Norman's room, she held to the hope that the Irish boy was in the kitchen. He would have the television on very loudly. He would be singing too in that funny growling voice. So much noise, it was no wonder he hadn't heard the bell ring.

'No one,' Maitland said coming back. 'Are you all right?'

'Yes.'

'He should have been here by now. May Stewart promised to send him back as soon as he came in. I'll check with her.'

When he went out into the hall, she took the bottle from her pocket. It lay in the palm of her hand and she turned it over with her finger. A little clear plastic bottle with the kind of cap you pushed down and turned, the kind hard for children to open because it held tablets or pills. It was empty.

He came back shaking his head. 'He hasn't come into the office this morning.'

It had not occurred to her Maitland might wish her dead.

'Why don't you lie down?' he said. 'Having come this far, it's worth waiting.'

'No.' If she lay down she would sleep and not waken again. They would find the bottle he had put into her pocket with its traces of whatever he had given her. Verdict, suicide.

'Maybe Norman's gone,' Maitland was saying. 'Gone off for good. I should have told you, but I wanted you to see how he reacted when I confronted him. Julian Chambers wrote to me about it. Naturally he was for calling in the police at once. I persuaded him to let me deal with it.'

'With. What.' She drew up each word separately out of herself.

He settled on the edge of the bed, unbuttoning his coat one-handed as he spoke. The heavy cloth slid open over his thighs. 'I gave him authority to set up a contingency account. A mistake as it turns out. He was contacting firms that weren't on our appeal list. Viv Law did publicity for one of them. She wondered about it. Mentioned it to

May Stewart, who told Julian. A word to the bank manager – Julian had been at school with his father – a quite unofficial check and there it was. Money in, money out. A simple clumsy embezzlement. As a stranger, our friend didn't realise how small a town this is . . . So you see it was all coming apart. Finishing . . . you can hardly keep your eyes open. If we give it another half-hour, you could lie here and rest . . .'

She shook her head. She must not sleep.

'I have a kind of notion that when he went to the Trust he had some ambition to succeed there,' Maitland said. 'It's not a large job, of course, and perhaps at first he imagined it was. And then, the truth is that whatever its size he couldn't really do it. If he hadn't realised that before, I'd guess getting a tongue-lashing from Viv Law made the point sufficiently. Sitting in this dreary place – Are you warm enough? If you lay down, I could put my coat over you . . . It wouldn't be impossible to feel sorry for him. No one to talk to. He must have felt the walls closing in.'

Me, Lucy thought, he had me to talk to. He could talk to me about a girl and the sad horrible things he made her do. How he had shared her with friends and how it had all gone wrong for him. Like her a piece of meat, I wasn't going to tell anyone. How could he have known some part of me was awake and how carefully it listened?

She wasn't mad. Even dying some stubborn part of her rejoiced at that. She had seen the scarred man and felt his hands on her throat.

'. . . not or hell that's there all . . . allright' – she sighed and was still.

Maitland got up and went behind her chair. She was too tired to turn her head. He laid his fingers on her forehead, their tips were cold, and gently massaged her temples with his thumbs. 'Poor darling, is it very bad?' Her body recognised the familiar comfort of his voice. It would be easy to give in and sleep. 'Even turning up for regular office hours was beyond him. The rewards of being honest come in small increments. They're real enough, but you need to be brought up to have a taste for them. They were a little subtle for his palate. All the same, just at first for him I suspect the words Gregory and Rintoul Trust had a ring to them. He stepped into it so easily . . . no effort required . . . all in one step like a daydream . . . that would suit nicely . . . The dreamer in the dosshouse.'

The murmur of his voice came more slowly and his hands lingered and lifted away. Her eyes drifted open in time to see him going out into the hall. He's pretending to answer the door, she thought. He wants me to think I heard someone knocking. But he won't come back. I wish I had been able to tell him it was all right, I don't mind dying. I dreamed there was a prison where no one had ever been imprisoned. In the morning, I told my dream to Maitland and he said, Some Christians believe that out of all creation no soul has ever been sent to Hell. Just that it exists is enough. He was telling me not to be afraid.

She had been alone for an endless time. Yet when Maitland came back he was pushed into the room so things must have been happening fast. The man behind held him by the upper arm. The second man crowding in past them didn't stop until he stood over her. She had never seen either of them before. There was a great noise, much of it made by Maitland who was shouting, 'Tell them who I am!' The man bent and put his face into hers so close she saw on the white of his eye a thin yellow line like a crack in porcelain. 'She's not about to say a thing.' His breath in her mouth was minty as if he had just taken a mouthful of toothpaste. From his cheek there came the tang of aftershave. He was a very clean young man. 'Don't touch her!' she heard Maitland cry out.

As the young man straightened and turned he held his right arm a little behind him so the knife in his hand was concealed. When she saw it she knew what was going to happen and it was very strange since she had thought it was she who was going to die. 'This is for my sister, you bastard,' he said and there was a scream of agony and

234

when he moved aside there was blood on Maitland's trousers between his legs.

He would have fallen down, but the man behind hooked a finger into each corner of his mouth and held him upright. Like that with his face pulled out of shape and the redness in his hair it would have been hard to tell him apart from Monty Norman. He wrenched his jaw from side to side but there was no way he could bite the fingers that held him up. The upper lip was drawn back and because the gums had receded the teeth seemed unnaturally long. The mouth made a clown shape but it didn't look at all like laughter, instead it began to stretch and narrow and gagging noises came out of it as if trying to tell her, 'I'm sorry' or even 'I love you.'

Or and most likely, 'Tell them who I am.'

And then the young man hid him again for an instant and when he moved back the knife was sticking out of the socket of Maitland's eye.

And even then and all the time and in all the days that were to follow she held to one thought.

She would never let them drive her back into the place of the mad.

BOOK EIGHT

The Heart's Affections

30

Some Christians believe that out of all creation no soul has ever been sent to Hell.

Though afterwards, almost at once, he had gone on, – But I expect that was declared a heresy by the Calvinists against the Arminians or by the synod of Carthage just after they condemned Pelagius. Too much mercy has always been heretical.

Driving into the city, she saw a freshening in the colour of the fields and thought before she remembered, I must tell Maitland there's a change towards spring. Storing things to tell him was as habitual as breathing. So much talk over the years. She hadn't ever said that she knew he was disappointed with his life, or asked why he dared to be, or told him how angry it made her. So much talk but not one word that told how something in him wanted to bring down all the world – himself – or that mirror image of himself which was her – the fading image of a girl who had walked with him hand in hand one summer's day looking at pictures hung on the railings in a park.

They had never talked.

Even now, and that would have been the moment for them, tears wouldn't come. Her discipline was complete. She had begun to impose it upon herself even in the moments before she lost consciousness.

I'll never let them drive me mad again.

The policeman in the hospital told her what she had taken was the same mix of tablets which killed Sophie Lindgren. If that was a mystery, let them solve it. Let them look for Monty Norman and the scarred man and the men who had killed her husband. She knew nothing. It was a doctor who told her, if you hadn't been sick that morning in your car, you would be dead.

Above Princes Street the castle on its hill lay like a cut-out against the sky. There's nothing up there, Maitland had said, the group of them standing outside Jenners looking up at it. It's a bit of theatre, just lathe and plaster and painted canvas, *that* wide. It's not any more or less real than the house in *Psycho*. The American couple laughing seemed almost half persuaded. Anyway, he said straight-faced, what could be more appropriate? This is the most schizophrenic city I know.

When she went into the gallery, Anne Macleod was nowhere to be seen. There were display cases with ceramics on shelves and past them to the rear a long room with no one in it though there was a table with two piles of typed sheets and a visitors' book lying open. She stood in the middle of the room and turning looked at the pictures carefully all the way round. They didn't mean anything to her, and since she had expected they would that was a disappointment. When she went up close, however, it was a man who had put his signature on them, and at the table she realised the typed sheets were catalogues, one for this man but the other for Beth Lauriston.

Carrying the typed sheet she went back to the front area and found a stair to an upper floor. It led to a high L-shaped room filled with space and light around a woman seated behind a table like the one in the downstairs gallery. It seemed there was no one else, but as the woman glanced up Anne Macleod came into view from the hidden part of the room, making a desultory progress along the pictures hung on the far wall.

On seeing Lucy she became perfectly still for a moment and then rushed across. Lucy let her hands be taken. 'Are you all right? I've thought about you all this time.' Her voice echoed shocking the silence. 'Blamed myself.'

'Yes, yes,' Lucy said softly.

She found herself being drawn towards the stair. 'I didn't know whether you'd be at home – or with relatives. I even tried to find out from the police. It was such a relief when you answered the phone – to hear your voice. I was in tears.'

Lucy drew her hands away. 'Could we stay here?'

'Why?'

'Just for a little,' Lucy said. In arranging to meet at the gallery, she had imagined it would be a busy place, but there had been no one downstairs. At least here there was the woman at the table.

'I have to talk to you.'

'I know,' Lucy said. She moved off, hesitating at one painting, stopping before another though she could not have said what was in front of her.

'I want to look after you.'

'I'm not mad.'

'That's not what I meant. You know it's not. I care about you.'

Lucy moved from that painting to the next, Anne following her.

'There's nothing you would want from me,' Lucy said, 'that I could give you.'

'A chance to love you.' And now her voice trembling she spoke as softly as Lucy, who looked round in a kind of fright at the word *love* – but the woman behind the table sat with her head bowed in just the same way as before.

'That's over for me.'

'You talk of yourself as if you were an old woman. He made you feel like that. You've lived your life seeing yourself through his eyes.' As Lucy retreated, still keeping up the pretence of looking at the paintings, the soft insistent voice stayed by her. 'You were unhappier than you knew. And if you stayed with him out of fear of being alone, aren't you alone now?'

Driven into the farthest corner of the gallery, Lucy defended herself. 'When you came to our house it was

241

Maitland I chose. You asked me to go with you then. I didn't. I didn't want to.'

'Oh, my dear.' She cradled Lucy's face in her hands. Over her shoulder Lucy saw the woman lift her head but without looking round. The private Lucy, Lucy Inside, thought, she must imagine we're having a lovers' quarrel, how tactful of her not to look! I would. 'That wasn't you choosing. Don't you know that?'

'Please.' Lucy gave her head the tiniest shake until she was free of Anne's hands.

'You had been at Monty Norman's flat. Who knows what he told you to do?'

'He wasn't there.'

'Would you remember if he was? If he came back after the other man left? If he'd told you to forget? How long had you been waiting when I found you. Ten minutes? An hour? You don't know what happened.'

'But what is that if it's not madness? To have him in my head, not to know.' And then the consequences of that. 'Was it me who put those tablets into Sophie Lindgren's drink? You can't tell me it wasn't. How can I ever know it wasn't?'

'Because she put them in herself. Because she was unhappy. Or maybe Monty Norman put them in. Maybe he hypnotised her and told her to do it.'

Consequences. 'I thought Maitland was trying to kill me. I thought he gave me the tablet. But what if I took them myself? You say I might have seen Monty Norman. Suppose he told me to kill myself?'

Anne Macleod stroked her arm. Her voice full of pity, she said, 'That isn't what I meant.'

'If he was in my head then, why shouldn't he be now?'

'No. Now is when you're free, my darling. Free of all of them. The only sure moment is this one.'

'Free? You're talking about my husband being *dead*.'

'Lucy—'

'How dare you say that to me? What do you think I am

that you can say something like that to me? I loved my husband.'

At that Anne Macleod gave a little cry as if she had been struck. She actually put a hand to her heart. As if checking the wound, the idea came unbidden to Lucy Inside, *like an actress*. My God! and she's the star – in spite of that plain face – and those awful glasses!

It was as if everything had been put into words. They looked at one another with the face of enemies and then Anne Macleod said, 'If you had gone with me that night, he would still be alive.'

If I look at this painting, Lucy thought, she'll stop being here.

And it did happen after a time.

I won't let them, she thought. It isn't any use you trying to make me feel guilty. I won't let that happen to me any more.

Every night she woke out of dreams in which she saw Maitland's mouth pulled out of shape.

'Do you like it?' a voice said. 'It's my favourite. Though for all the wrong reasons, I suppose.'

It was the woman who had been sitting at the table. Beyond her a man was taking up one of the catalogue leaflets, an elderly couple were leaving.

'You've been studying it for such a long time.'

'I'm all right,' Lucy said.

'Yes. I didn't mean—'

'Only I'm not, of course. My husband died in an accident.'

Tell them who I am, he had said.

'Oh, dear.'

'He left me money. Much more than I expected. I'm going to buy a painting.'

'I think that's a lovely idea.'

'He left a will listing it all. He had accounts in different building societies. If he got money, some unexpected windfall, he would open an account – he didn't take money out. There must have been better ways he could

243

have invested it. But he wasn't good with money, not really. Like a peasant, do you know what I mean?'

'I'm like that myself. Lots of us are.'

'He must have been afraid of not having any. I never knew that about him. Though I knew he had been poor when he was young. He even bought a flat. People rented rooms in it. That was why he had the keys for it.'

The man who had been working his way round had come to a halt beside them. 'Ah . . .' he said, 'I do like this one.'

'Thank you,' the woman said.

'I mean it, Beth. I'd like to buy it.'

'Well, you can see it's not for sale,' the woman said.

'You wouldn't like to reconsider? I seriously covet this one.'

'Sorry, Tony.'

'Pity. Worth a try. You're depriving the gallery of its forty per cent.'

'Fifty,' the woman said.

'Usurers.'

While they talked about that, Lucy stared at the woman and then turning to the painting saw what had been in front of her all this time.

It was winter. A sky of grey clouds, the paint laid on in thick scoops. By some trick of perspective the boy was clear and close yet you knew he was out there and the ice under him was creaking; knew it, of course, from the look on his face. The look not of anything as simple as fear, though fear was there, the fear of dying, but of excitement too, of being more alive than you'd ever been.

A dark-complexioned boy with a thick tangle of black hair.

And, of course, you knew about the ice and all the rest of it – the lighthouse out of sight over the hill and the way the current ran that would carry you under the ice to the far end where you'd be held until the spring came. And found yellow as the grass. You knew about it because you'd been told.

244

Maitland. Maitland as a boy, or rather the way someone who knew him as a man might imagine he would have been then.

The woman had gone with the man to look at another painting. When they were finished and he was gone, Lucy went over to the table where she had taken her place again.

'I like that painting, too,' she said, 'the one of the boy.'

The woman raised her head reluctantly. She's decided I'm a nuisance, Lucy thought, or perhaps unstable.

'Not to buy.' Lucy made herself smile. 'I heard you say it's not for sale. It's just that it's so real, I felt it had to be true.'

'Thank you.'

Lucy laid the catalogue leaflet she had been carrying down beside the pile of them. 'Do you use your married name?'

'I'm not married.'

' "Beth Lauriston" . . . It's a name you remember. I suppose that must be an advantage.'

'I could have kept my name, that's not why I didn't marry,' the woman said, with a little smile that came and went at once.

'Weren't you ever in love?'

The woman tilted her head, peeping up. She's here on her own, Lucy thought, and wary in case I'm going to make a scene of some sort.

'My painting has been everything to me.'

'That's hard for me to imagine. All I ever wanted was to be married and have a family.'

'That must be nice.' And as Lucy stared not understanding, 'Having a family.'

'Oh, yes,' Lucy said. 'My little girls.' For a moment, tiny hands were warm in hers and then they were gone. She couldn't see their faces. 'So even if a man wanted to marry you, you would have said no.'

'There weren't so very many offers,' the woman said, and the little smile appeared and went again.

'Even if he was ready to give everything up and marry you.' When the woman frowned, Lucy pointed back towards the painting of the boy on the ice. 'Did someone tell you about it? I meant what I said about it seeming real. As if it really happened and he told you about it.'

'I wouldn't want to talk about that,' the woman said.

'Is he dead?'

'Who?' The word came as a gasp, with something of fright in it.

'When you said that. I wondered if he was dead.' And Lucy pointed back towards the painting.

The woman instead of answering turned a page of the book which lay open on the table in front of her.

'And now he's dead. You're sad, but you kept something of him alive. At least you have the child.'

She didn't take her eyes from Lucy, turning a page without looking at it.

Touching wood, Lucy thought, as if I was someone who had come to lay a curse upon her. 'The painting, I mean, imagining him as he must have looked as a child.'

'I'm sorry,' the woman said, 'you've got it wrong. That's a painting of my son.'

When in the summer term the University held a memorial service for Maitland, Lucy was almost sure Beth Lauriston hadn't come. By that time, however, she could not remember her face very clearly, so it was possible she was there.

Afterwards some of the staff walked with her to her car, shook hands, said the last meaningless things. On impulse, she pulled over at a quiet spot on the campus road and walked down to the edge of the loch. It was warm and the water was blue that had been grey and ringed with ice all winter. She picked up a stone, a flat one that you might send skipping across the water, and then held it forgotten in her hand. At some point during the service, she had been trying to remember the last time Maitland made love to her. She had been trying to remember as much as she could, but the minister's voice made it hard to concentrate. It had seemed just then desperately important not to lose any of it, since that was the last time anyone would make love to her. The holiness of the heart's affections. The phrase had run in her head. The words not meaning anything. A quote from somewhere. Holiness. Heart. Affections.

When she heard the noise of someone coming down the slope to her, she didn't mind that it was Sam Wilson. It was unlikely she would see him again.

'I don't want to interrupt,' he said. 'It was just that during the service, I wasn't thinking of Maitland's work or how distinguished he was. It was something that happened just after I'd come here, and seeing you I felt I needed to tell you. When I came at first I was an academic warden. In one of the halls over there.' Across the loch white concrete blocks crouched beneath soggy hills drying out under the sun. 'Dreadful narrow little rooms like passages. So depressing. I think that makes people cruel. There was a ringleader, of course. And the one they picked as a victim. In the lavatories graffiti on the walls. "Rodney is scum". Does that sound silly? I thought he would end by killing himself. I told Maitland. He was . . . very fierce. I do believe he saved that boy's life.'

As he finished, his voice broke and he began to sob. Unable to stop, he made angry little chopping gestures with his hand.

'I'm so ridiculous,' he wept. 'You've been remarkable. Wonderfully brave. I'm so *sorry*.'

'It was kind of you.' She wondered if she should lay her hand on his arm, but wasn't sure he would want that.

'You must miss him so much.'

It came into her mind that now Maitland was dead there was no one to remember her as a girl. While he was alive, and whether or not he wished it to be so, that young girl and how she had looked being in love was held in memory.

She doubted if Sam Wilson would understand any of

that, and so instead she said, 'The place where he died was so awful. Such a shabby room.'

'I'm a Christian, you know. Not that I push it at anyone. But I find it does help.'

'If it wasn't for the thorns and the poor hands with nails through them. I wish instead of the Cross we had a symbol of the cave and the rock rolled away. That would be a better thing to have in our thoughts.'

'I never heard Maitland say that.' Like a boy he wiped with his fingers at the tears drying on his cheeks.

'No,' Lucy said, 'I thought of that by myself.'